"Zoe, what is it?"

She lifted her gaze to his. "I confided to my aunt that you… turn me on."

Seth gulped. "And she said…"

"That I should ask you if you want to have temporary sex because maybe some sex is better than no sex and we're two consenting adults and why shouldn't we just enjoy ourselves?" She paused to take a breath. "If you want to. You might not, because I really am leaving and so there's—"

"You're kidding, right?" His heart hammered and breathing became a chore.

Her response was almost a whisper. "No. Not kidding."

"Zoe, I would crawl over broken glass to spend even one night with you."

"You would? Even though this can't go anywhere?"

"Even then. Are you saying you want that? You want me to make love to you?"

She swallowed. "Yes, please."

A COWBOY'S HOMECOMING

THE MCGAVIN BROTHERS

Vicki Lewis Thompson

Ocean Dance Press

A COWBOY'S HOMECOMING
© 2019 Vicki Lewis Thompson

ISBN: 978-1-946759-81-8

Ocean Dance Press LLC
PO Box 69901
Oro Valley, AZ 85737

This is a work of fiction. Any resemblance to actual persons, living or dead, business establishments, events, or locales is entirely coincidental.

Cover art by Kristin Bryant

Visit the author's website at
VickiLewisThompson.com

Do You Take This Cowboy?

1

A B&B located on the outskirts of Eagles Nest, Montana suited Seth Turner perfectly. He could hang his hat there for a few days without drawing attention. Better yet, it wasn't owned or operated by a McGavin.

He planned to introduce himself to his recently discovered relatives and use his Christmas break to get acquainted. *Surprise! I'm the nephew and cousin you didn't know you had.*

Could turn out great... or not. Either way, he had kinfolk he needed to meet. The prospect made his gut tighten, though. He'd prefer to ease into it.

His mom, God rest her soul, had done him a favor when she'd chosen to give him her last name instead of his father's. Flying under the radar, he could scope out the small town and announce his connection to its most prominent family once he had the lay of the land.

Snow and holiday traffic had lengthened the drive and it was suppertime when he reached the turnoff to the B&B. He'd texted the owner, Maureen Stanislowski, to make sure she'd hold his room.

His truck handled the entrance road to The Nesting Place fine, but the tires sprayed snow as he plowed his way through the drifts and finally parked in the small lot reserved for guests. The three-story Victorian looked mighty inviting with lights shining from the windows and a huge wreath decorating the front door.

White lights along the roofline and the porch railing illuminated a woman in a lavender parka with a fur-lined hood attacking the snow on the walkway with a shovel almost as big as she was. She put her back into it, flinging snow off the path with admirable efficiency.

Grabbing both of his tightly packed duffels, he hopped out of the truck and forged a path in her direction. "I hope you're not doing that for me."

She paused and leaned on the shovel, her rapid breaths clouding the air. "Are...you...Mr. Turner?"

"Yes, ma'am, and I—"

She took a couple of seconds to steady her breathing. "Aunt Mo wanted the walk shoveled for your arrival. I volunteered."

"That's hospitable of you, but I can manage. That's plenty good enough."

"Now that I'm out here, I might as well finish." She hefted the shovel. "Guests will be coming back from dinner in town and they'll be grateful for a cleared walkway."

"Then let me do this last part for you." He turned and started for the truck. "I'll just put my stuff back in the—"

"Oh, no, I can't let you shovel." The blade bit into the snow with a crunch.

"Why not?" He set the bags in the truck and shut the door.

"You're a guest." Snow flew in a rhythmic pattern.

"That may be so, but I surely can't stand around while you shovel." He retraced his steps, packing the snow down with his boots.

She paused and gave him a once-over. "You're a cowboy, aren't you?"

"Yes, ma'am. And I'd be much obliged if you'd let me complete this job for you."

She smiled. Great smile. With dimples. "Aunt Mo's been educating me about cowboys. She says you take the term *gentleman* to a whole new level."

"So you're not from around here?"

"No. And much as I appreciate your gallant offer to shovel the walk, that's not how we treat our guests at The Nesting Place."

"But I—"

"Sorry, Mr. Turner." She moved the shovel out of reach.

"Please call me Seth." Since he'd just passed his thirty-first birthday, he was touchy about being called *Mr. Turner* by a woman who looked younger than he was, a woman determined to shovel her own snow.

"Okay, then, Seth, there's only a little more to do and I'm perfectly capable of handling it. In fact, I love shoveling snow."

"You *do*?"

"Yes, so you wouldn't want to rob me of that pleasure, would you?"

"No, ma'am, but I—"

"Then why don't you go inside and get registered? I'll bring in your luggage when I'm done."

"Now that's where I draw the line." She'd outfoxed him. He couldn't very well wrestle her for the shovel, but he'd be damned if she'd carry in his bags, especially since the one full of gifts for his relatives was heavier than a load of bricks.

He retrieved them from the truck and returned to the scene of battle. "I still think I should—"

"Please give it up, Seth." Her response was breathy, but she didn't break rhythm. "I've got this."

He heaved a sigh. "I can see that." Might as well accept defeat gracefully. "I'll go on in, then."

"Excellent. Welcome to The Nesting Place."

"Thank you, ma'am." He strode quickly up the walkway.

"Name's Zoe!" she called after him. "Zoe Bradford!"

"Nice to meet you, Zoe Bradford!"

"Same here, Seth Turner!"

He grinned as he took the porch steps two at a time. She was both self-sufficient and quick on the draw, a lethal combo that pulled him in. He wanted to know more about this snow-shoveling woman.

After wiping his boots on the holiday mat, he slung one bag over his shoulder so he could open the door. Then he stepped inside and closed it behind him.

"Mr. Turner! You've arrived!" The B&B's owner came toward him, beaming.

"Yes, ma'am." He glanced around at the miniature Christmas trees, the staircase railings festooned with red bows, and the poinsettias tucked into every spare corner. "Beautiful place."

"I'm glad you like it."

"I surely do." The interior of the house, coupled with the aroma of cinnamon and pine, wrapped him in a hug that nearly unmanned him. He swallowed past the lump in his throat. His mother would have adored this.

Maureen Stanislowski didn't look anything like his mother, which helped keep him steady. His mom had been tall and willowy, but Mrs. Stanislowski was short and compact with a head of curly gray hair and a no-nonsense manner. That last part was like his mom, come to think of it.

"Thank goodness you made it safely! Not a good night to be on the highway."

"It wasn't all that bad. And I really wanted to get here." He set down both bags and took off his Stetson.

"So you said." She waited, her expression expectant, as if there had to be more to it than that.

The cheerful holiday surroundings and her kind gaze coaxed him to tell at least a part of the truth. "My mom loved Christmas and she... passed away fourteen months ago."

"Oh, honey. I'm so sorry."

"Last Christmas sucked." He took a shaky breath. Admitting to his grief always required more air than he normally had in his chest. "I needed a change of scenery this year."

"I'm sure you did, son. Eagles Nest is a good choice."

"I hope so."

"I moved here after my husband died. I miss him like the devil this time of year, but I'm surrounded by cheerful folks who love celebrating the holidays. It lifts my spirits considerably."

"Makes sense."

"Let's get you checked in."

"I met your niece outside. She offered to carry my luggage in for me."

Mrs. Stanislowski laughed. "That sounds like Zoe." She slid into the chair behind an antique desk and consulted the computer sitting on it.

"She seems like a go-getter."

"No kidding. I keep telling her she doesn't have to tackle all the physically demanding jobs around here." She tapped on the keyboard and eyed the monitor. "But she does, anyway."

"She's pretty good at clearing away snow."

"She's from Wisconsin." She said it as if that explained everything. "Can I have your card, please?"

He dug it out of his wallet. "Are Wisconsin folks born knowing how to shovel?"

She chuckled. "Feels like it." After running his card, she handed it back. "Wisconsin kids, at least the ones in my family, are taught that snow happens and you need to move it out of the way.

We counted the days until we were old enough to use the blower."

"Do you have one here?" He wouldn't have been so determined to help if Zoe had been using a blower.

"You know, I do, but it's noisy. Ruins the ambiance so I don't get it out often. Besides, my niece loves shoveling snow the old-fashioned way."

"She said that, but I thought she was kidding."

The door opened and Zoe walked in, pink-cheeked and triumphant. "Done!" She pulled off her gloves and tucked them in the pockets of her jacket. "I put the shovel around back, Aunt Mo."

"Thank you, sweetheart. The Franklins and the Smiths will appreciate the effort."

"That's the idea." She flashed him a dimpled smile. "Keep the guests happy."

"You're doing a great job so far, although I would have been even happier if you'd let me shovel." He couldn't stop looking at her. She was so full of life, so ready to take on whatever came her way. He'd never met someone who loved shoveling snow.

"I'll make a note of that. Since you're a guest, I should try to accommodate you." She threw back her hood to reveal wavy red hair cut short, almost like a guy would wear it.

Except when he looked in those sparkling brown eyes, he'd never mistake her for a guy. The challenge in their depths was uniquely feminine. At first he'd taken her for early twenties, but she was probably a bit older.

"Mr. Turner, here are your keys."

He broke eye contact with Zoe and accepted the keys.

"The one with the blue fob unlocks the front door. The green one is for your room."

"Got it. And before I forget, where can I find a fast-food place with a drive-thru?"

"The Burger Barn has a drive-thru, but they're not particularly fast."

"And the burgers at the Guzzling Grizzly are way better." Zoe unzipped her parka. "I was actually planning to invite my aunt to dinner at the GG tonight."

Her aunt blinked. "You were?"

"Absolutely. My treat. It's Friday night, so they should have music, right?" She turned to him. "Would you like to join us?"

He took a quick breath. "I don't want to impose." Not to mention going to the Guzzling Grizzly meant potentially running into his cousin Bryce, who co-owned the place.

"It's not an imposition. It's an invitation. You'll love the food and the atmosphere is wonderful."

Maybe Bryce wouldn't be around. And he'd certainly enjoy the company. "Then I accept. Thank you."

"And I appreciate the offer, sweetheart, but can I take a raincheck?"

"Well, sure, but—"

"I'm ready for a bowl of soup and a movie on TV." She smiled. "You two go have fun. Dinner at the GG would be an excellent introduction to Eagles Nest. You can take my SUV."

"Beg your pardon, ma'am, but unless Zoe's opposed to it, we'll go in my truck."

"Fine with me." Zoe slipped off her parka and hung it on a hook by the door. She was a slender woman. If not for that, the rounding of her belly might not have been quite so noticeable.

He glanced away. Wouldn't do to be caught staring.

She turned and gestured toward the stairs. "I'll show you to your room."

"That's okay. Just tell me where—"

"No worries. It's right next to mine. While you settle in, I'll freshen up and meet you downstairs."

"Sounds good." He grabbed both duffels and followed her. He was no expert on the subject, but that bump sure looked like she was carrying a baby. And she wasn't wearing a ring, either. Gave a whole new spin to this energetic woman's story.

2

Zoe changed into a yellow sweater her mom had sent last week. Hip-length and loose, it disguised her pregnancy, unlike the knit shirt she'd had on before. Seth had noticed her baby bump—no big deal—but she might as well keep her secret a little longer from the good folks of Eagles Nest.

After putting on fresh lipstick, she headed downstairs. Seth hadn't appeared yet, but Aunt Mo was still at her desk working on the computer.

Her aunt glanced up. "That sweater looks good on you."

"Thanks. Are you working on something you can leave for me so you can go relax with your soup and movie?"

"I'm almost finished." She went back to typing. "I realized today I hadn't ordered the favors for New Year's Eve. There. Done." She closed the laptop, rolled back her chair and stood. "I'm glad you came up with this plan." She lowered her voice. "I'm sure he could use some company. He said his mom died fourteen months ago."

"Oh, dear. She must have been fairly young."

"Probably. He looks about thirty or so." She glanced past Zoe to the stairs. "Ah, Mr. Turner. Is the room to your satisfaction?"

"Yes, ma'am. I like it very much. And you're welcome to call me Seth."

"I will if you'll call me Maureen."

"It's a deal." He glanced at Zoe. "Ready?"

"Just have to get my coat." She started toward the door.

"I've got it." He beat her to the punch, lifting her coat from the hook and flipping it open.

Her aunt hadn't been kidding about gentlemanly cowboys. Turning, she slipped her arms into the sleeves and caught a whiff of shaving lotion. "Thank you." She zipped up. "Aunt Mo, want me to bring you anything?"

"A piece of pumpkin pie would be lovely, if they have any left."

"I'll ask first thing. See you soon." She whisked out the door Seth held for her and flashed him a smile. "I could get used to this."

"Nothing wrong with that." He tipped his hat and called out a goodbye to her aunt before following her out and closing the door. "My mom was big on manners."

Her heart squeezed. "Aunt Mo told me that she passed."

He met her gaze. "Life doesn't always turn out the way we want."

"It doesn't, and some things hit harder than others." Such sad eyes. "I hope this trip will help."

"I hope so, too." As he descended the steps beside her, he turned up the fleece collar of his jacket. "Thanks for going with me tonight."

"You bet." She pulled up her hood. "I don't know about you, but I'm starving."

"Worked up an appetite clearing the walk?"

"Guess I did."

"Super job, by the way."

"Thanks."

"Your aunt confirmed that you love doing it."

"There's a Zen quality to shoveling. It's also a great upper body workout and good for the heart." She left the walkway and took the narrow groove he'd created during their debate about snow removal.

"That applies to mucking out stalls, too." His boots crunched through the snow as he followed her.

"I'm pretty sure I'd rather shovel snow."

"Don't knock it 'till you've tried it." He reached around her and opened the passenger door. "Come spring, snow won't be an option. Horse poop is forever."

She laughed. "Words to live by." When he helped her into the truck, she thanked him. His mom had probably taught him to assist ladies into his vehicle, and the physical contact was... lovely.

He also might be treating her with kid gloves because he'd noticed her baby bump. Until last week, when she'd entered her fifth month, her body hadn't looked much different. Only her folks and Aunt Mo had known. Well, and the OB/GYN in Milwaukee and the one at Eagles Nest General.

Her folks had agreed to tell friends who asked that she'd gone to Montana to help her Aunt Mo at the B&B. But there would be no hiding the evidence from those who saw her on a regular basis here in Eagles Nest.

Made sense that people would be curious about a woman having a child with no significant other in sight. She'd rather offer a simple explanation than leave them to speculate.

Seth started the truck and country music came through the speakers. He switched it off.

"That's okay. You can leave it on."

"I'd rather talk to you." He backed out of the parking space and pulled onto the entrance road.

"When you put it that way, I'd like that, too. Although I'm growing fond of country music, much to my surprise."

"You didn't like it before?"

"I didn't think I did. But everybody around here loves it, and after hearing it for a month, I've become a fan.'

"That's how long you've been here? A month?"

"Yep. My OB/GYN and I figured I could stay in Milwaukee until I hit my fourth month without anyone guessing I was PG. I left after Thanksgiving." She watched his reaction.

Clearly he wasn't surprised, but he took a few seconds to respond. Then he gave her a quick glance. "I had a hunch you were pregnant. "

"I had a hunch you had a hunch."

He laughed. "Yeah, but I wasn't going to say anything."

"Would you rather not discuss it?"

"I have no problem discussing it. Whether we do or don't is totally up to you."

"Then let's talk about it."

"Okay."

"You'll be the first person I've told besides my parents and Aunt Mo."

"Whoa. I'm honored, but why me?"

"You noticed. So far nobody else has."

"You don't owe me an explanation just because I noticed."

"That's very true, but until this past week I wasn't showing much, so it wasn't an issue. As time goes on I'll attract more curious glances. People will have questions, even if they don't ask them. Don't you have some?"

"Sure I do, but—"

"That's perfectly natural. I'm not wearing a ring and there's no guy around. I'd rather be upfront about the situation instead of acting like it's something I'd rather not discuss, or worse yet, something I'm ashamed of."

"Then the father isn't... in the picture?"

"Not if I can help it. I broke up with him when I found out I was PG. I'd rather he never found out."

"Why?

"He would expect me to abort the baby."

"You're sure of that?"

"Oh, yeah. He mentioned his aversion to having kids several times. We always used protection. Evidently there was a failure."

"He couldn't force you to have an abortion."

"No, but I'd rather not begin that ugly conversation."

"What about his financial responsibility? You didn't get pregnant by yourself."

"My parents mentioned that, too, and he would probably pay, grudgingly."

"Kids aren't cheap."

"I know, but I have resources. If he helped financially, my child and I would have a connection to him. I don't trust him. He could be nasty and resentful. No telling what awful things he might say to my little kid if he got the chance."

"If he's so terrible, why did you..." He paused. "Never mind. It's none of my—"

"He was a bad habit I should have broken much sooner. Discovering I was pregnant was my wake-up call. My folks ran into him with his new girlfriend recently. He's moved on."

Seth didn't comment, but a muscle in his jaw flexed. "So you'll shoulder the financial burden in addition to the emotional one of raising a kid?"

"Yes. Gladly."

"But... if he or she doesn't have a dad..." He exhaled. "That's problematic." His statement rang with the certainty of someone with first-hand experience.

Not hard to figure out why. "I'll take a wild guess that you were raised by a single mom."

"I was."

"Did you miss not having a dad around?"

"Yes."

"But isn't no dad better than a horrible one?"

He adjusted his grip on the wheel, leaned back and stretched his arms. "I couldn't say. I didn't have either."

Way to go, Zoe. "I'm so sorry. I invited you to go out for a fun dinner and I'm totally mucking it up with my personal drama." She took a deep breath and exhaled. "Can we start over?"

"I'm the one who should apologize. This is a hot button for me, and I—"

"Which is exactly why we should banish it from the discussion. Those lights ahead are Main Street. Let's drop this subject and just go have a nice meal in an awesome venue."

He let up on the gas. "Got here quicker than I expected. I don't want to pass the Guzzling Grizzly."

"Don't worry. It's at the far end of town. It'll be on your left."

"Not much traffic."

"Stores close at six."

"Even during the Christmas season?"

"I was surprised, too. Eagles Nest is unique."

He slowed the truck to a crawl. "Sure is pretty with the lampposts done up and the garlands hanging over the street."

"The holiday is big here. I was afraid I'd be homesick, and I am, a little. But all this plus Aunt Mo's beautiful decorations make up for not being with my parents."

"Couldn't they come out here to visit you?"

"We talked about it, but Aunt Mo refuses to charge them for a room and this is her second busiest holiday after Fourth of July. She'd lose revenue, and when the house is full she doesn't have much time to sit and chat with my folks."

"I'll bet she's grateful that you're around to help."

"She's said as much. I'm just grateful for her, period. I couldn't ask for a better safe harbor. I take up one of her income-producing rooms, too, and she won't accept any rent money. I work for her full-time, but I'm still not convinced that I do enough to—"

"You can't reduce it to money. I heard the love in her voice when she talked about you. I saw how she hugged you before we left. Does she have any kids?"

"No. She married an older man. As my mom says—older man, lower sperm count."

He laughed. "Your mom said that?"

"She tells it like it is." She pointed out the historic two-story building ahead of them. "Guzzling Grizzly, coming up on your left."

"I see it. Wow, that parking lot is jam-packed. No wonder traffic's light. They're all here."

"Quite a few are. Bryce McGavin and Nicole Williams are performing tonight. Have you heard of them?"

"I have, in fact."

"Do you have any of their music?"

"Some."

"Aunt Mo has it all. We like to play it while we work. The recordings are great, but there's nothing like seeing Bryce and Nicole live. Oh! A spot just opened up. If you get in there fast, maybe you can—"

"I'm on it." He swung quickly into the lot and slipped the truck neatly into the vacant space.

"Score! You're gonna love the GG, Seth. Everybody raves about their McGavin's Pale Ale. I haven't tasted it, obviously, but you could."

"But if it's their brew, why don't they call it Guzzling Grizzly's Pale Ale?"

"Probably because Rory McGavin crafted it and he deserves the credit. He spearheaded the idea of brewing beer on the premises."

"It's a new venture then?"

"Yep. Started about six months ago, I think. Rory's a fun guy. Great Scottish accent. The time I came here with Aunt Mo, he and his brother Aleck were tending bar, and they went heavy on the brogue because it's such a crowd pleaser. We decided to sit at the bar just so we could listen. I laughed until my sides hurt."

"Where did they pick up a Scottish accent?"

"They grew up in Scotland. They came over this year to visit their aunt and cousins for the first time."

He sucked in a breath and started coughing so violently that he fogged the window.

Zoe laid a hand on his arm. He was quivering. "Seth, are you okay?"

"Yeah, yeah." He coughed some more. "Swallowed... wrong." He cleared his throat. "So these guys... just came over?" His voice was raspy from the coughing fit.

"I'm sure there's more to the story than that. Aunt Mo said it made for a lively summer for the McGavins."

"I'm sure it did."

"They're a terrific family. I hope you get to meet a few of them while you're here."

"I'll make a point of it."

3

Holy hell. As Seth walked into the Guzzling Grizzly with Zoe, he held it together with difficulty. The McGavin brothers had welcomed two cousins from Scotland? Well, guess what? The odds were two to one that those cousins were his effing *half-brothers*.

One or both could be in this bar calmly serving McGavin's Pale Ale, oblivious to the dramatic info he possessed. His presence, once announced, would change everything they thought they knew about their family unit.

His heart pounded and sweat trickled down his spine. Rory and Aleck. Would they look anything like him? Would they spot him and immediately figure it out?

Long ago he'd concluded that his green eyes and dark hair were compliments of his father because his mother was blonde with gray eyes. He'd confirmed his assumption when he'd found a few snapshots tucked into her diary. He was the spitting image of Hamish McGavin.

His anxiety about meeting his aunt and cousins was nothing compared to the gut-churning prospect of coming face-to-face with his half-brothers. He tugged down the brim of his hat to give him some measure of protection as he snuck a quick glance toward the bar.

A woman with pink and purple streaks in her hair was dispensing drinks along with a dark-haired guy. Couldn't see the color of his eyes from here.

"What do you think?" Zoe turned to him with a smile that quickly faded. "Seth, what's wrong?"

"Nothing." He scrubbed a hand over his face. *Make up an excuse, doofus!* "See that woman at the table near the bar? She's with a balding man who's wearing glasses."

"That's Virginia Bennett. Her wedding venue brings the B&B lots of business."

"She looks something like my mom. Startled me a little bit."

"More than a little bit, I think. You looked panic-stricken."

"Sorry." He dragged in air and tried to get a grip. Zoe had removed her parka and draped it over one arm, while he still wore his sheepskin coat. No wonder he was sweating.

He took off his coat and hat and turned away from the bar. "I haven't done much socializing this past year. Didn't feel like going out. I guess I was disoriented for a minute."

"We don't have to stay if it's too much for you."

He was tempted to run. But that would be cowardly. He was many things, but a coward wasn't one of them. "No, I want to stay. I can see why you like it. The place is loaded with character." And likely McGavins. He'd been prepared for cousins. Half-brothers, not so much.

"It's even better once the music starts." She sounded so sweet and hopeful. "Bryce and Nicole should be out any minute."

"Can't wait." Another challenge, but doable. His first guaranteed McGavin sighting.

"Hi, Zoe!" A middle-aged woman wearing a red Guzzling Grizzly t-shirt hurried over to greet them with menus in hand. "I see you brought a friend tonight."

"Jenny, this is Seth Turner. He's staying with us over Christmas. He's never been to Eagles Nest, so I wanted to start him off here."

"Of course you did! Welcome to the Guzzling Grizzly, Seth."

"Thank you, ma'am. It's as amazing as Zoe told me it would be. The Christmas decorations look real nice."

"Wait'll you tuck into the food. And hear Bryce and Nicole play. Would you like a table or a seat at the bar?"

"A table, please." He was staying clear of that bar, beautiful though it was. The carved wood and the etched mirrors were draped in ribbons, pine boughs and holly. Ordinarily he'd love to take a stool at a bar like that. But the cowboy behind the bar could be Rory or Aleck and he was not ready.

Jenny clutched the menus to her chest as she surveyed the crowded room. "Oh, good! A two-top by the dance floor is being cleared. How's that?"

"Great!" Zoe gave Seth a look of triumph. "Our luck is running." She followed Jenny over to the small table on the edge of the dance floor.

Nothing subtle about this spot. He'd be able to see Bryce just fine. And Bryce could see him. That was okay. Bryce wouldn't be looking for a man who might be related to him.

That was true of his half-brothers, too, so he should relax. Nobody knew he existed... yet.

Originally, he'd planned to acquaint himself with the town for a couple of days and then pay a visit to his Aunt Kendra. The way things were playing out, though, he might not have that luxury.

Jenny handed them each a menu. "Your server will be over shortly. In the meantime, can I get either of you something from the bar?"

"A sarsaparilla for me, please," Zoe said. "Oh, and Aunt Mo asked if I'd bring her a piece of pumpkin pie. Do you know if there's any left?"

"I'll put a slice aside if we still have some. How about you, Seth? Something to drink?"

"A McGavin's Pale Ale, please."

"Good choice." Jenny peered at him. "How long have you been in Eagles Nest, son?"

"Arrived less than an hour ago."

"Then you probably haven't met very many people."

"Just Mrs. Stanislowski, Zoe, and now you."

"One person you have to meet is Aleck McGavin."

"Why's that?" His stomach pitched.

"You really remind me of him, especially your eyes."

Words stuck in his throat. He couldn't have come up with a response if someone had stuck a gun to his head.

Zoe jumped into the silence. "I see what you mean. I didn't realize it until you said that. Too bad he's not here tonight."

The knot in his stomach eased. The dark-haired guy behind the bar wasn't Aleck. Thank God for small favors.

"Yeah, you won't see Aleck or Rory in here tonight. Their folks are flying in from Scotland and the boys drove to Bozeman to fetch them."

The air left his lungs. Shoving back his chair, he stood. "Left something in the truck. Be right back." He bolted out the door.

An icy breeze slapped some sense into him and he skidded to a halt in the middle of the parking lot. What a crazy move, running out like that. He dragged in a breath that froze his innards. Then he clouded the air with a generous supply of curse words.

"Seth?"

He turned.

A parka-clad Zoe held out his coat. "Better put this on."

"Thanks." He took it and pushed his arms into the sleeves. "Sorry about that."

"I assume you didn't leave anything in the truck?"

"No." He turned up his collar against the cold wind.

"Listen, we can leave." She pulled the lapels of her parka together. "I didn't bring your hat, but I can pick it up when I tell them we won't be staying."

"But you need dinner."

"So do you. Normally we don't offer guests an evening meal, but—"

"You don't need to this time, either." His heart rate had returned to almost normal. "We'll go back in. I'll pretend I left my cell phone."

"Something's freaking you out, though."

Should he come clean? He hesitated. She'd trusted him with her story. Was he ready to trust her with his?

He cleared his throat. "I'm not visiting just because I need a change of scenery this Christmas." He paused and took a breath. "Turner was my mother's last name. A couple of months ago I read my mom's diary and found out my father is a McGavin."

"A McGavin?" She stared at him, wide-eyed. "Are you saying Kendra McGavin's late husband is your—"

"Not Ian. His older brother, Hamish."

"Holy horse poop."

"Exactly." He managed a smile. "Couldn't have said it better myself." She'd lightened the mood, too. He was grateful.

"Does Hamish know about you?"

He shook his head. "Mom's diary says he left for Scotland before she knew she was pregnant. She never told him about me."

"Did she tell anyone?"

"Only her folks, who disowned her."

"Ouch."

"She left the area, but she kept track of Ian, who stayed in Eagles Nest, married Kendra and fathered five sons. After reading that, I decided to come down and meet my aunt and cousins."

"Who also don't know you exist."

"Not yet."

"Oh, Seth." She moved closer and gripped his arms. "No wonder you hightailed it out of there. Now I understand why you acted weird when I told you about Rory and Aleck."

"My half-brothers."

"And on top of that, your father is coming—"

"I didn't know if he was dead or alive, let alone on his way to Eagles Nest...." His breath caught. "Zoe, is there a chance he and his wife have booked a room at the B&B?"

"No."

"Are you sure?"

"Absolutely sure. If Aunt Mo had booked a room for Aleck and Rory's folks coming all the way from Scotland, she would have been beyond excited. She would have told me, especially if they were coming in tonight."

"So where will they stay? There aren't any hotels in town. I checked. The Nesting Place is it."

"Since your dad is Kendra's brother-in-law, I'll bet she's invited them to stay at Wild Creek Ranch."

He nodded. "Makes sense."

"So what would you like to do?" She'd said it as if she wanted to help.

Come to think of it, he could use an ally. This caper would be far more intense than he'd counted on, but for tonight, he had a short reprieve. He sucked in more of the icy air. Then he held out his hand. "Let's start with a nice meal and some good music."

4

Zoe stepped into the welcoming warmth of the GG and paused to take off her coat. Seth followed her in and shrugged out of his.

Before his confession in the parking lot, he'd had her sympathy, but now he had her admiration, too. Instead of smoothing the way for this meeting with the McGavins by sending a letter or an email to Wild Creek Ranch, he'd chosen to show up in person. Gutsy move.

Bryce and Nicole had taken the stage, hamming it up with their rendition of the Johnny Cash and June Carter Cash hit, *Jackson.* Conversation stopped as the crowd gave its full attention to the performance.

Seth laid a hand on her shoulder and leaned close to murmur in her ear. "Let's wait 'till they're done."

His warm breath tickled. But that wasn't all it did. Nobody had warned her that the hormone overload of pregnancy could make her long for things she had no business wanting.

This too will pass. Her grandmother's favorite saying. Zoe held onto it until her inconvenient response to Seth ebbed. No point in adding layers to an already complicated situation.

Her toes tapped out the lively beat of the song while she studied Bryce for any features he and Seth had in common. Body build was one. Evidently broad shoulders and narrow hips ran in the family.

But the way McGavin men carried themselves was even more distinctive than body type. They all exuded quiet confidence. Seth had done that, too, until he'd been knocked sideways by the unexpected news of his half-brothers and the imminent arrival of his father.

He'd regained his moxie, though. Although Bryce claimed all his attention, his steady breathing and relaxed posture held no trace of his earlier panic. Maybe telling her his story had helped a little.

Getting a glimpse of his first McGavin might have relieved some of his anxiety, too. Who wouldn't be proud to be connected to a talented guy like Bryce?

The song ended and Seth applauded enthusiastically along with the rest of the crowd. "He's damned good. *They're* damned good."

She smiled. "Glad you came?"

"Definitely. Let's head back to the table."

A server arrived shortly after they were seated and took their order as Bryce and Nicole chatted with the audience.

"Any two-steppers out there?" Nicole called to the crowd.

The audience responded with a chorus of *yes, ma'ams*. No surprise, there. *Yes, ma'ams* flowed like water in Montana. Even Seth joined in. He might be new in town, but clearly he was at home in a country bar.

"Well, we've got a great number for the dancers in the room. It's *I Need You*, our version of the hit by Faith Hill and Tim McGraw."

Seth pushed back his chair. "Zoe? Can I interest you in a little two-stepping?"

"You want to dance?"

"Don't you? You were excited to get a table next to the dance floor, so I figured—"

"I thought you wanted to keep things on the down-low."

"I do, but if I don't grab a chance to dance to their music, it's a missed opportunity."

"Okay, then. I'd love to."

"Great." He stood and helped her out of her chair. "I'm a little rusty, so bear with me."

"I won't be able to tell if you're rusty or not. I've never danced to country music."

He chuckled. "I notice that didn't stop you."

"It looks like fun."

"Then let's go have some." Slipping his hand around her waist, he twirled her onto the floor.

She was unsure of herself at first, but then she caught his rhythm and her feet knew what to do.

"Nice."

She glanced up. "What is?"

"Getting out on the floor. I've missed it. And knowing Bryce is playing... that's special."

Pressing his palm into the middle of her back, he executed a tricky maneuver.

She managed to keep up with him. "I think the rust is coming off your dancing shoes."

"You're not doing so bad, yourself. You've never tried country dancing before?"

"No, but I love other types of dance and I'm a fast learner."

"A fast learner and an expert with a snow shovel." He spun her under his arm. "What else are you good at?"

"Yoga. I have a studio in Milwaukee."

"Did you close it when you came out here?"

"Heavens, no. My assistant Danica is running it, but I'm still handling marketing and the financials. We're in constant touch." She followed him through a series of twists and turns that left her pulse racing. "What are you good at?"

His laughter was slightly breathless. Comforting to know he had to exert himself, too. "Shoveling."

"That's it?"

"And some cowboy stuff."

"Like what?" Although the town was chock-a-block with cowboys, she'd never questioned any of them about the tasks involved.

"The usual. Saving maidens tied to the tracks and riding off into the sunset."

"Yeah, yeah." She rolled her eyes. "Besides that."

"Anything to do with the horses. My specialty is training foals. Best job in the world."

"I can imagine. On a ranch?"

"Yep. Near Glacier Park. Beautiful country." As the song ended, he twirled her one last time and pulled her close for the first time. "We did it."

"Sure did." Breathing hard, she looked up at him. Embracing while pregnant. A whole different experience.

He tightened his grip slightly and his expression grew tender. "All three of us."

Her cheeks warmed at the intimacy of that remark. "Um, yeah."

"Thanks for dancing with me." He released her slowly. "Guess we'd better see if our food's here."

"Might be." She led the way back to their table. "Not yet. I can't wait for you to taste their burgers and fries. The GG is famous for them." She slipped into the chair he pulled out for her.

"Read the reviews online." He scooted the chair in as Bryce and Nicole began singing a soft ballad.

"You didn't ask around, find out if anybody had been down here?"

"I decided not to broadcast my plans."

"In case it didn't go well?"

"Something like that. I just said I was taking a road trip. My buddies aren't the type to press for details, especially since Mom died. They've been good about letting me work through it."

"Then I'm the only person in the world who knows why you're here?"

"For now."

"Have you considered not going through with it now that your father is on his way?"

He hesitated. "I did for about two seconds in the parking lot." He glanced toward the stage. "Would have been a shame if I had." Returning his attention to the table, he picked up his beer. When he caught her looking at the mug, he held it out to her. "Would you like a sip?" He glanced at her belly. "That shouldn't be a problem, right?"

"Not a tiny sip." She accepted the mug and took just enough to coat her tongue. A mouthful probably wouldn't hurt her baby, but she wasn't taking any chances. "Mm."

"Like it?"

She savored the taste, rubbing her tongue on the roof of her mouth. "Love it. I predict great things for Rory's brewing operation."

He sampled the beer. "Yeah, that's good. What does Rory look like?"

"He's a redhead, a lighter shade than mine. The Scots call it ginger."

"A redhead. Huh. Must take after his mother. Did they come over here together?"

"No. Rory arrived in the spring. Then Aleck visited him over Fourth of July and now they've both applied for dual citizenship."

"Wow. They must have fallen in love with Montana."

"The way Aunt Mo tells it, they each found a woman they couldn't live without."

His eyebrows lifted. "Fast work."

"Aunt Mo credits the feel-good vibe of Eagles Nest. And the name of the town. She swears it awakens the nesting instinct in people."

"Do you think she's right?"

"Hey, look at me. I got in the family way and chose to head to Aunt Mo's cozy B&B, appropriately called The Nesting Place."

"But you also said you'll go home after you have your baby."

"Oh, absolutely. I want to be close to my folks, and I can take my baby to the studio with me. It's perfect. I may even expand the business after I get back. The extra revenue would sure help while raising this munchkin by myself."

"Right."

Oh, yeah. Touchy subject. Time to change it. "Montana's beautiful, though. I'll try to see more of it before I leave. Any suggestions?"

"You might want to head up toward Glacier."

"I've seen pictures. It looks gorgeous."

"There's nothing like being there, though. The ranch where I work rents out a few cabins."

"They rent cabins and raise horses, too?"

"The cabins help pay for the horse raising. Then again, the foals are a big draw, so it's a profitable combination."

"What does it involve, training foals?"

He held up both hands. "You don't want to get me started."

"GG super burgers and amazing fries coming up!" Their server arrived with their food. "Another Pale Ale or sarsaparilla for you folks?"

"I'm good," Zoe said.

"Me, too, thanks."

"Alrighty. Just signal if you need anything." She hurried to a neighboring table.

"I'd love to hear about training foals." Zoe picked up a fry. "These days I'm fascinated with babies of all kinds. You might have some tips for me."

"I doubt that training a foal is—"

"They're newborns, too."

"With hooves and teeth."

She laughed. "There's that. But I'd be interested in your process. I'll bet there are commonalities."

"Okay." He scooped up his burger. "First off, I make sure I'm there for the birth and that I have plenty of chances to touch the foal. That creates a bond." He took a generous bite.

"See? Touch is universal." And dancing with him had made her keenly aware that she hadn't been touched a whole lot in the past few months. The full body contact he'd created by pulling her close at the end of the dance had filled a yearning she hadn't acknowledged.

He put down his burger and started in on his fries. "The foals love it. If their first experience with humans is the pleasure of being stroked and fondled, they're so much easier to work with."

Whoa. This wasn't an academic discussion of raising young creatures. Instead he was using words like *stroked* and *fondled.* She should change the subject. She didn't want to. "Tell me more."

He warmed to his subject, and *warmed* was the operative word. His enthusiasm for his work shone in his eyes and vibrated in his voice. Clearly he loved his job, which evidently was very hands-on.

She figured he was good with his hands. Even the way he ate, corralling his burger neatly without dropping any of the contents, demonstrated that. She'd learned when they'd danced that his hands were work-roughened, a new experience for a city girl.

She'd never made love with a man who had callouses at the base of his fingers. How would it feel? But she had no business thinking about Seth in that way. Or any other man. Cutting her mental vacay short, she concentrated on her juicy burger and crisp, salty fries.

When they'd finished the meal, he glanced at her empty plate and his. "Do you want dessert?"

"No, thanks. I'm stuffed. You go ahead if you want."

"None for me." He looked over at the stage, where Bryce and Nicole strummed the opening chords of the next number. "Let's have one more dance before we leave."

She was ridiculously happy that he'd asked. Probably another bad sign. She should say no. But... "I'd like that."

5

The tune was a Bryce and Nicole original, *Whenever I Waltz with You,* a slow, dreamy number suitable for lovers.

Since the pace was easy-going, Seth could hold Zoe a little closer than was technically correct for a waltz. And he did, because he wanted to.

Brushing against her gently rounded belly was a constant reminder of why he needed to keep his distance. But she felt so good in his arms.

She waltzed like a pro, but that wasn't why he was enjoying himself so much. He flattened his palm against her back and absorbed her warmth as he breathed in the sweet scent of her perfume. "You've done this a few times."

"A few."

The husky note in her voice told him she might be affected by their closeness, too. Was that so terrible? It wasn't like they were going to take it any further.

The sensual friction created a predictable result, though. His jeans pinched and her breathing grew uneven. Harmless enough.

The song ended. He gazed into her eyes. "Time to head back."

"Right." She took a shaky breath. "I promised Aunt Mo a piece of pie."

"Better get that delivered." A hand at her waist, he escorted her to their table as Nicole and Bryce announced a short break.

Seth got the attention of their server, who came over with the check and left to fetch the pie. As he pulled out his wallet, Zoe took a small zippered purse from her coat hanging on the back of her chair. He glanced at the purse. "This one's on me."

She shook her head and unzipped it. "I invited you."

"And helped me keep my cool when things got dicey." He laid his hand over hers. "Please put that away."

Her dimples flashed. "Only if you'll let me get the next one."

"Okay, I will." Her assumption that they'd share another meal pleased the heck out of him. He put money on the table and helped her on with her coat.

As he adjusted the drape of the hood, he brushed the warm nape of her neck. A glimpse of her creamy skin beneath a fringe of silky hair tempted him to lean down and press his mouth against that tender spot. He didn't.

"Are you two leaving, then?"

He glanced in the direction of the speaker and met the curious gaze of Bryce McGavin on his way over from the bandstand. Slipping quietly away from the GG was no longer an option.

"Oh, hey, Bryce." Zoe's nonchalant tone gave nothing away. "I'd like you to meet Seth Turner, who's staying with us for the holidays. He arrived hungry so I brought him here."

"Excellent call." Bryce stuck out his hand. "Pleased to meet you, Seth. I didn't think you'd been in here before. I hope we made a good impression."

"Sure did. Your music is amazing." He shook Bryce's hand. First familial contact. The guy had a firm grip. "I've really enjoyed it."

Bryce grinned. "Good. I'd hate to think you were leaving because you couldn't take another set."

"Zoe promised to bring her aunt a piece of pumpkin pie."

"Maureen loves her pumpkin pie."

"Do you make it here?"

"Nope. We import almost all our baked goods from Pie in the Sky down the street, but they're closed this time of night, so we're the only source. Gives us plenty of business."

"I'm guessing your music does, too."

"It does, and for that I'm grateful."

"Great venue for it. The folks raving online about the Guzzling Grizzly know what they're talking about." He focused on breathing as normally as possible and gradually his heart stopped racing.

"So you heard about us online?"

"I did."

"Have you ever been to Eagles Nest before? Because you look very familiar. That's why I came over."

Jenny walked by and paused briefly. "He looks quite a bit like Aleck."

"That's it! I wish Aleck was here so you two could meet."

"That would be exciting, all right." Zoe ducked her head and concentrated on zipping her parka.

Keep it casual. "I hear Aleck's from Scotland."

Bryce nodded. "That's a fact."

"I recently found out I have relatives in Scotland." He wanted to give Bryce a piece of the puzzle even though now wasn't the right time for a full reveal.

"Hey, maybe you two are related! Wouldn't that be wild?"

"It surely would."

"But not impossible. It's a smaller world than we think." He glanced past Seth. "Here comes Renata with Maureen's pie, so I'd better let you two go. I hope you'll come back, though, Seth. You need to meet up with Aleck and find out if you two are second or third cousins."

"That would be interesting."

"Wouldn't it? I'll look forward to seeing you again. Thanks for bringing him in, Zoe."

"You bet. I talk up this place all the time."

"And I'll definitely be back." Seth exchanged another handshake with his cousin, grabbed his coat and hat and followed Zoe out the door.

She waited until they were safely out in the parking lot. "That was the weirdest conversation I've ever listened to."

"Only because you know what's going on behind the scenes." The conversation with Bryce had shifted his attention back to his reason for being here, which had effectively cooled his jets. "Thanks for not giving me away."

"It's not my place." She glanced at him as they walked toward the truck. "You're a cool customer, Seth Turner McGavin."

"How so?"

"I had trouble keeping a straight face when you suggested to Bryce that you might be related to Aleck."

"I hope he'll realize later I was intentionally giving him a hint. It's all I could do, though. For one thing, he's in the middle of a performance. For another, he's not the one who should hear it first." He opened her door, helped her in and rounded the truck to climb behind the wheel.

"Who is the person who should get the info first?"

"I'd planned on starting with Kendra, but my dad's arrival will make that tougher." He put the truck in reverse and backed out of the parking space. "I mean *Aunt* Kendra. I've practiced calling her that but I'm not used to having relatives."

"I guess your mom's folks don't count."

"That's for sure. They were so mean to her that I have no interest in befriending them, ever." He drove out of the lot and cruised down a deserted Main Street.

"I can understand that."

"My mom worked hard to make up for it, though." He focused on the wintry road ahead of him. "She did a fine job, but I still longed for that Thanksgiving dinner with fifteen or twenty relatives around the table. Or even just my dad."

"I can see why you were excited to discover you had an aunt and a bunch of cousins here."

"I was, but judging from what I found on the town's website, they're a tight-knit bunch. I'm concerned that their closeness might mean they won't accept an outsider like me because—"

"Aunt Mo said they were thrilled when Rory and Aleck showed up."

"But they were born into the family."

"So were you." She placed a hand on his arm. "Everything I know about the McGavins tells me they'll welcome you with open arms."

"I hope you're right." The warmth in her voice and the pressure of her touch had rekindled the heat that had seeped away during the interlude with Bryce. He tamped it down.

She gave his arm a squeeze and put her hand back in her lap. "It's probably a good thing that Bryce came over to talk with you."

"I agree. Once I got past the shock of speaking to him face-to-face, we had a normal conversation. I like knowing I won't hyperventilate whenever I meet one of my relatives."

"That is nice to know, but it wasn't my point. His arrival changed the dynamic between you and me."

Ah. She wanted to discuss that. Okay. "Yes, it did."

"Don't get me wrong. I had a wonderful time dancing with you tonight, but my hormones are doing the jitterbug because of this pregnancy."

"You'll have to forgive my ignorance. I don't know if that's good or bad."

"Neither. Just inconvenient. Fortunately, I've managed to channel my frustrations by taking on most of the physical work around the B&B. It's a perk I hadn't counted on when I came out here."

"You mean things like shoveling snow?"

"Yep. And cleaning guest rooms, scrubbing the kitchen counters, or anything that requires a lot of elbow grease and won't complicate my life."

"Understood." He took a deep breath. "I won't lie. Dancing with you affected me. But I wasn't going to do anything about it, Bryce or no Bryce."

"I didn't think you would." He wasn't a cad like her ex.

"That said, I suspect I'll remember our last dance for a very long time."

6

Now that Zoe had dispensed with the subject of their mutual attraction, a decent segue to a more neutral topic proved elusive. Evidently Seth couldn't come up with one, either.

After a few minutes, he turned on the radio. Dolly Parton was in the middle of *I Will Always Love* You. After a couple of bars of that, he switched it off again. "Do you clean all the rooms?"

"Yes, I do. Why?"

"How long does it take?"

"Usually a big chunk of the day."

"Then what?"

"I check in with Danica, catch up on QuickBooks, help Aunt Mo set up for Happy Hour, run a load of linens through the washer and dryer, things like that."

"What if I helped you clean? I'm a pretty good hand with that kind of stuff. Could I buy you a couple of free hours?"

She laughed. "I don't picture Aunt Mo letting a valued guest clean rooms, but let's say she's fine with it. Why do you need a couple hours of my time?"

"If you're willing, I'd like to book a short trail ride for the two of us with Aunt Kendra tomorrow."

"You're going to tell her?"

"Not yet. I just want to meet her and a trail ride seemed like the way to do that."

"What if you run into your father?"

"I'll take that chance, but I doubt I will. No reason for him to be down at the barn when she's dealing with paying customers. Would you like to go along?"

"Sure, but I—"

"Wait. I just thought of something. Is it okay for you to be on a horse?"

"My Eagles Nest doctor told me I could before I'd even asked. I guess she expects all her patients to be horse people. But I'm not."

"You don't ride?"

His shocked disbelief made her smile. "I live in the city. I don't know anybody with horses."

"Makes sense, then. Do you have anything against the idea?"

"No. I just don't know how."

"That wouldn't be a problem on a short trail ride. What do you think?"

"It might work. But first we'll have to see if Aunt Mo is okay with letting a guest clean. I'll ask when we get back."

But when she walked through the front door of the B&B, the place was quiet. No sound of a TV filtered out from her aunt's private quarters. She tossed back her hood and spied a note on the desk. Putting down the to-go box, she picked it up.

Zoe—Couldn't keep my eyes open. If you brought pie, please leave it in the fridge. I'll have it tomorrow. See you in the morning. I hope you two had a fun evening. Love, Aunt Mo

She handed the note to Seth, took off her coat and hung it up. "I'll ask her first thing in the morning."

Nudging back his hat, he scanned it quickly. "I'll make the reservation and if she nixes the plan, I'll cancel one of the horses."

"I'm hoping she doesn't." She walked back to the desk and picked up the to-go box. "Knowing the situation, I'd love to be there when you meet Kendra."

"I kind of thought you might."

"I need to stick her pie in the fridge. Thank you for a lovely evening. I'll see you in the—"

"I'll wait and walk up with you."

"Thanks, but you don't need to."

"A gentleman walks a lady to her door."

She gazed at him. His manners tickled her. "I'll be right back." When she returned, he'd taken off his coat and hat.

"After you." He gestured toward the stairs.

She lowered her voice. "This time of night, most of the guests are asleep, so I take off my boots before I clomp up those stairs." Leaning against the antique reception desk, she nudged them off, leaving her in her sock feet.

"I will, too, then." He laid his coat and hat on the desk, took the spot she'd vacated and removed his boots. "After you."

She started up the stairs, aware of him following her. "Breakfast starts at seven."

"You help with that?" His voice rumbled softly in the muted light of the stairwell.

"Yes."

"Then you have to be up before seven."

"I do, but I promise I'm very quiet. You won't hear a thing."

"Don't worry about me. I'm a ranch hand. Getting up early is what I do." His hushed delivery made ordinary comments sound like pillow talk.

"But you're on vacation." She came to the top of the stairs and started down the hall. "You could sleep in."

"Tell that to my body clock." He walked beside her down the hall.

And speaking of bodies, his didn't suck. She came to his door and paused. "This is your stop."

"I'll come back to it."

"My door is right there. Five steps away." She swept a hand in that direction. "Thanks again for tonight. I'll see you downstairs in the morning."

He grinned. "I'd press the point and insist on taking those five stops, except that would be dorky."

"Yes, it would."

He held her gaze as the laughter in his eyes morphed into something more intense. "I wasn't kidding about that last dance. It was special."

Awareness curled in her stomach. "It was. Goodnight, Seth."

"Goodnight, Zoe."

She turned and walked to her door. Before she opened it, she glanced back. Seth was right where she'd left him, watching her.

She almost blew him a kiss. Nope. Wrong message. Instead she waved and ducked into her room. Great guy. But she wasn't in the market, especially for a Montana cowboy.

* * *

The next morning a little past seven, a dashingly handsome Seth was in the breakfast room eating and chatting with the other guests. He'd come downstairs with a fresh shave and hair damp from the shower.

His denim Wranglers and crisp white Western shirt with pearl snaps looked new. His boots gleamed from an application of polish.

His arrival should have been no big deal, but when he'd caught her eye and sent her a dazzling smile, she'd spilled the coffee she'd been pouring into the urn. The eggs had burned while she'd watched him make friends with the other guests. When he was on his game, he had charm to spare.

Pancakes weren't as tricky as scrambled eggs, and she managed to create a stack of fluffy, lightly browned ones without incident. She carried in a loaded platter along with a pitcher of warm syrup.

Seth left his chair and met her before she made it to the table. "I can pass those around for you."

She glanced at him and couldn't help smiling. He was just that beautiful. "You do realize this is my job."

"I asked your aunt if I'm allowed to help and she said I could."

"Funniest thing, she agreed that you could help with the cleaning, too."

"She mentioned that to me."

"She said it's in your genes to be helpful." Zoe handed over the platter and the syrup. "Clearly she understands cowboys better than I do."

"Stick with me and I'll teach you everything you need to know."

She resisted the urge to fan herself. "I'll keep that in mind. Since you're handling the pancakes, I'll go back and slice up some more fruit. The bowl's almost empty."

She retreated to the kitchen and leaned against the counter while she caught her breath and calmed her racing pulse. Either he was the most potent male she'd ever come across or she was awash in hormones this morning.

Laying a hand over the curve of her belly, she leaned down. "You have much to answer for, little one. Once you get here, we'll have a talk."

"Ah, Zoe, there you are." Aunt Mo bustled in. "I've been thinking about Seth's request."

"If you want to change your mind, that's okay with me. This is a busy time, and—"

"I'm not changing my mind. You keep refusing to take time off, but I think it would be good for you. I can hold down the fort here this afternoon and evening if you want to hang out with Seth."

"That's sweet, but I also need to check in with Danica today and post an update on the website, so I—"

"Then go take care of that now. Once you and Seth finish cleaning the rooms, you'll be free to relax."

She hesitated. "Breakfast isn't over. I'm not sticking you with the cleanup."

"Sweetheart." Her aunt cupped her face in both hands. "I can handle it. In another four months, you won't have the luxury of a carefree afternoon and evening with a handsome cowboy. Take advantage of this chance."

"Okay." Wrapping her arms around her aunt, she gave her a tight hug. "Thanks."

_Z_

After Zoe found Seth in the breakfast room and told him the new plan, he wanted to give her aunt a big hug. He didn't know her that well, though, so he had to settle for a simple thank you. Then he stayed after breakfast and helped her with cleanup.

As he finished loading the dishwasher, she came into the kitchen, her arms full of table linens. She paused, her gaze sweeping the spotless counters. "You know, I used to regret not having a daughter. Now I also regret not having a son."

His chest tightened. Better treat it like a joke and save them both from an embarrassing emotional reaction. "It so happens I'm available for adoption."

"Wonderful news. I'll start the paperwork right... whoops, I'm losing some of this load." A napkin landed on the floor.

"Here, let me help." He picked up the napkin, scooped the bundle out of her arms and headed for the laundry room.

"Thanks. If you'll shove them in the washing machine, I'll take it from there."

"Any stains?"

"None this morning. Evidently you have experience with laundry, too."

"My mother was the ranch cook." He shoved the linens in the front-loading machine. "We only used tablecloths for special occasions, and she put me in charge of the laundry end." He closed the door. "What temperature?"

"Cold. Soap's on the—"

"I see it." He put some in the dispenser and set the dial.

"Does my heart good to watch a manly man efficiently operate a household appliance." Her voice softened. "My Bobby could handle any chore, too."

Seth hit the power button and straightened. "I was taught by the best." He met her gaze and looked away. If they weren't careful, they'd both end up blubbering.

Zoe arrived in the nick of time, flushed and smiling. "Enrollment's up at the studio."

Her aunt beamed. "Excellent."

"I know! Usually the rush comes in January when New Year's resolutions kick in. But my *Give Yourself the Gift of Yoga* campaign is working great. Danica's thrilled. We decided to add another class to the schedule."

"Good to hear, sweetheart."

"I slipped in a quick yoga workout while I was talking to her." She turned to Seth. "In other words, I'm ready to clean rooms if you are."

"Let's do it."

"You're getting a top-notch assistant, Zoe." Her aunt glanced at him. "Thanks for helping out."

"Anytime, Mrs. Stanislowski."

"I think you need to start calling me Aunt Mo."

"I'd be honored."

Moving closer, she patted his cheek. "You're a good man. Just like my Bobby. Now I'm off to do a grocery run." She bustled out of the kitchen.

Zoe's dimples flashed. "You have a fan."

"And I'm hers. She's terrific."

"Yep, she's amazing." She glanced at the kitchen clock. "What time is our ride?"

"One, but we should probably grab something to eat before then."

"Stopping at the Burger Barn on our way out there is our best bet. And FYI, they have chicken sandwiches, too."

He laughed. "I'm a guy. I've been known to eat burgers five days in a row."

"Which you can totally do here, but we'd better get moving. The cleaning supplies are in a closet under the stairs. Extra linens are there, too." She started out of the kitchen.

"Are we stripping beds?" He fell into step beside her.

"Only two out of the eight. We change sheets every third day of a guest's stay. And if they hang up their towels, we keep that same three-day schedule for those, too."

She crossed the reception area and opened a door into a cedar-lined closet. A clipboard hung on the inside of the door. Unhooking it, she handed it to him. "Old school tracking system. I offered to put the info on a tablet, but Aunt Mo wasn't crazy about the idea."

"A clipboard fits the ambiance better than a tablet."

Zoe laughed. "Good point. We'll start with the two rooms where we'll do a complete linen change." She handed him a pile of sheets and added a couple of towels, then a couple more before eyeing the stack of linens he was balancing. "Can you take two more?"

"Sure."

"Okay, then. Second floor, opposite end from ours is where we'll start. I'll bring the vacuum and the cleaning supplies."

"I'm on my way." Anchoring the top towel with his chin, he climbed the stairs and turned right.

"This really will go faster." Zoe walked up beside him. "I usually have to make two trips, sometimes three, to get everything up here." Setting down a plastic caddy and a canister vac, she pulled a key out of her pocket. "It's nice that you're so tall."

"Glad you approve." He waited while she tapped on the door, opened it and called out a greeting.

"Good. we're clear. Go ahead in and set the sheets and towels in the rocker by the door."

"Will do."

She followed him in with the vacuum and the cleaning caddy. "I suggest one of us take the bathroom and the other one the bedroom. Which do you want?"

"Either."

She smiled. "Aunt Mo wasn't kidding about top-notch help. Okay, since I doubt my rubber gloves would fit you, I'll take the bathroom. Have you used a vacuum like this before?"

"Yes, ma'am."

"Then I'll leave you to it. If you finish before I do, I'll open the next room so you can keep moving. Any questions?"

"Just a comment. I can see why your yoga studio is doing so well."

"Oh?"

"You're good at creating a plan of action."

"Thanks. I like to think so. Create a plan and commit to it. It's worked for me so far."

"Clearly it has." And he admired the heck out of her ability to focus. Her no daddy plan would probably work out just fine, too. She'd thought it through and made her decision. Just because he regretted never knowing his dad didn't mean her kid would.

But the churning in his gut every time he noticed her baby bump told him there was also a chance her plan had a serious flaw.

* * *

Working with Zoe turned out to be fun. Like him, she took satisfaction in a job well done but she wasn't a perfectionist. If sharing this job with her every morning meant they could spend a couple of daylight hours together, he'd be all for it.

She coordinated washing the sheets and towels with the cleaning routine so by the time they returned the supplies to the closet under the stairs, the folded sheets and towels were ready to go in, too.

As he handed them to her, a middle-aged couple loaded down with shopping bags walked into the reception area. Gus and Tricia Langsdorf. Nice people. During breakfast, he'd learned they were in the room next to his.

Zoe welcomed them with a smile. "Hey, there, Mr. and Mrs. Langsdorf! Can I get you two anything? A pot of spiced tea? Some Christmas cookies?"

"No, thank you, honey. And like I mentioned yesterday, you can call me Tricia." She took off her furry coat. "After being here forty-eight hours, it feels like a home away from home. You and Maureen are family, now."

Gus nodded. "What she said." He gestured toward Seth. "And this guy reminds me of our son David, always ready to lend a hand." He turned to him. "Looks like you've been helping Zoe with her chores."

"Yes, sir, I have. I surely appreciate being compared to your son. It's a shame he couldn't come home for Christmas."

"He should get leave in January. In the meantime, the Nesting Place is a good alternative for us. Better than sitting at home when he can't be there."

"We picked up some gifts for him and the shopping wore us out," Tricia said. "Thought we'd go upstairs and rest for a while before heading out to lunch."

"Great idea." Zoe didn't look at all surprised to hear that. "Your room's all set and the house is quiet so you won't be disturbed."

"Then we'll just toddle upstairs." Tricia glanced at her husband. "Ready, Gus?"

"Ready, dear." He followed her.

Seth lowered his voice. "Are they really going to take a nap at ten-thirty in the morning?"

"Maybe. It's more likely they're going to fool around, though."

His eyebrows lifted. "You think they came back to have sex?"

"I do. I noticed early on that many of our long-married guests take naps during the day and I thought it was an age thing. I mentioned it to Aunt Mo because she's the same age and she doesn't nap. She clued me in that most of the time, it wasn't about sleeping."

"I'll be darned."

"Evidently a change of scenery puts them in the mood."

"Huh. Learn something new every day." But he could have done without the information. In his struggle to keep his relationship with Zoe strictly platonic, he didn't need to be reminded that other people in the B&B were having sex.

8

Zoe closed the door to the cleaning closet and glanced at Seth. "That's it! You're great to work with. Thanks for pitching in."

"Happy to. I had a good time."

"Yeah, me, too. It's not often I find someone who works at my pace."

"I had to put on the afterburners."

"I doubt that. You can pretend to be a laid-back cowboy, but I don't get that vibe from you."

"What do you get?"

She hesitated. "Restless energy searching for... I'm not sure what, exactly."

He gave her a crooked smile. "That makes two of us."

"But you'll know it when you see it?"

"God, I hope so. Anyway, we need to shove off pretty soon."

"I just need to go change into my boots and then we can leave." She headed for the stairs.

"And I need to fetch my coat and hat." He followed her. "Do you have a hat?"

"Nope. I've thought about buying a Stetson as a souvenir, but I haven't done it yet."

"Not even a baseball cap?"

"Not even that. If the sun's too bright, I'll wear my shades."

"I guess that works. At least it's not summer." He ducked into his room. "Meet you downstairs."

"I'll be right there."

He hadn't arrived by the time she came down, but Aunt Mo was home with her groceries. Zoe helped her carry them into the kitchen.

"Eagles Nest is jumping!" Aunt Mo put down her bag. "Are you two going out for lunch before the ride?"

"We'll swing through the Burger Barn and eat on the way out to the ranch."

"Good plan. Oh, and before I forget." She reached in her coat pocket. "I got Seth a ticket to the talent show. Do you think he'd want to go?"

"I have no idea, but I'll ask. Let me see if he's down yet." When she walked into the reception area, he was descending the stairs carrying his shearling jacket and his Stetson.

Heat settled in her core. If she kept on the move, she could ignore her inconvenient reaction to him, but whenever she stopped long enough to take in the arresting picture he made…

He glanced up and smiled. "I've been on the phone with Aunt Kendra. She'll be about ten minutes late. She went into town to pick up some pies and got caught in traffic."

"Aunt Mo said it was a madhouse this morning. She picked up a ticket to the Christmas talent show tomorrow night if you'd like to go."

"Thanks! I sure would. I saw something about it online but I didn't know if out-of-towners could go."

"Anybody can. Aunt Mo bought our tickets last month because she didn't want me to miss out. I'm glad she thought of picking up one for you before they're all gone."

"I appreciate it. How much do I owe her?"

"Not a thing, son." Aunt Mo walked in. "It's my pleasure." She handed him the ticket. "You'll have a good time. It's rumored that this year we'll have a pipe band as one of the acts."

"Bagpipes?"

"That's right. Aleck McGavin plays the pipes and his brother Rory accompanies him on the snare drum. Badger's threatening to join in now that Aleck's taught him the basics of the pipes."

"There's a person in town named Badger?"

"He's more like a force of nature," Zoe's aunt said. "You'll know what I mean when you meet him."

"I look forward to it. My mom was fond of bagpipe music so I've heard a lot of it."

"Then you'll feel right at home. Hey, don't let me keep you two. The line for the Burger Barn is long anytime of the year and it'll be even longer five days before Christmas."

"Thanks, Aunt Mo." Zoe put her arm around her aunt's shoulders and kissed her on the cheek. "Are you sure you won't need me for anything else today?"

"Not that I can think of, sweetie. Go have fun. Just let me know if you'll be here for dinner."

Seth put on his jacket and helped Zoe with hers. "I was planning to ask Zoe to have dinner with me and you're welcome to join us."

"That's lovely of you, Seth, but some of my guests enjoy lingering over Happy Hour so I indulge them."

"Alrighty, but the offer stands whenever you think you can get away." He put on his hat and touched two fingers to the brim.

"I'll keep that in mind," she called after him.

Zoe stepped out on the porch and squinted. "Bright out here." Pulling her sunglasses from her pocket, she slid them on.

"I wrangled you a hat."

"You did?"

"Since I was talking with Aunt Kendra, I asked if she kept any spares around. Our barn does, so it was a good bet she would, too. Sure enough, she has a couple of western-styled ones and some adjustable caps with the Raptors Rise logo on it."

"Thank you."

"You're welcome." He put the truck in gear and headed for the main road. "Which way do I go?"

"Make a right on the main road once you see the town welcome sign, make a left just beyond it, then an immediate right."

"Thanks. Got it." He braked the truck, checked for traffic and pulled out on the two-lane. "Speaking of Raptors Rise, would you be interested in going there with me after we finish the ride? It's close by."

"That's run by Zane McGavin, right?"

"Right. He might not even be there, but at least I'd like to see the place. It sounds amazing."

"Then let's do that."

"Perfect." He passed the town's welcome sign, made a left, then a right, and pulled into the line for Burger Barn's drive-thru. "We're almost to the ordering whatchamacallit. What would you like?"

"I'll take the chicken sandwich, please."

He nodded. "Fries or onion rings?"

"Fries."

"To drink?"

"Lemonade would be great."

He pulled up next to the gizmo with the speaker, rolled down the window and repeated her order times two.

"You got the exact same thing?"

He rolled up the window and followed the next vehicle in line. "That's what I wanted, too."

"Really?"

"Yep." He turned to her and smiled. "Freaky, huh?"

"A little bit." She reached in her jacket pocket, took out her zippered wallet and handed him a twenty.

He glanced at it. "I'll—"

She shook the bill. "We had an agreement. I'm sure cowboys always keep their word."

"Yes, ma'am." He sighed and took the twenty. "They do. Then I've got dinner."

"If you insist. Are you planning to brave the Guzzling Grizzly again tonight?"

"That partly depends on how things go at Wild Creek Ranch. But I wouldn't mind having an alternative. Is there one?"

"The Eagles Nest Diner. Family-friendly, hearty food, cushy booths. You get the idea. You won't spend the equivalent of a Stetson there."

"Doesn't sound nearly as exciting as the Guzzling Grizzly."

"No, but there's a good chance the GG will be chock-full of McGavins, including your father. Then again, maybe you're ready to storm the castle."

"Not exactly." He moved the truck another car-length closer to the pickup window. "I'm trying to imagine how I'd feel if I'd fathered a kid without knowing it and discovered the fact thirty-one years later."

"I'm guessing he'll need some time to process the idea."

"In his shoes, I would. I can't expect him to throw his arms around me first thing."

"This may be an obnoxious question, but do you have proof?"

"I have my birth certificate, which would put me in the right time frame, although he's not listed on it. And then there's my mother's diary. The diary should do the trick. She tucked a few snapshots in the pages of the two of them."

"Where are you keeping the birth certificate and the diary?"

"In a waterproof zippered pouch behind my seat. I wanted it on hand whenever I might need it."

"I get that. And, look, we're almost at the window."

"So we are." He pulled the truck in close and paid the kid who leaned out to take his money.

Zoe took the change he handed her and tucked it back in her purse. Then she happened to glance in the rearview mirror. "Seth."

"What?"

She took off her shades and peered more closely at the man sitting in a large black pickup. "I'm pretty sure that's Ryker McGavin behind us."

"Yikes."

"Yep, it's him, all right. Aunt Mo introduced me to him one day in the grocery store. He's ex-military and… imposing."

He deposited their drinks in the twin cup holders in the console and handed her the bag of sandwiches. "He's giving me the stink-eye."

"Because you—"

Ryker hit the horn and Seth jumped. "Why'd he do that? He can't know who I am."

"He knows you're the guy holding up the line."

"Oh, jeez." He took his foot off the brake and pulled forward.

"My fault. I just—"

"It's okay." Stepping on the brake, he stuck his head out the window and waved. "Sorry about that, buddy!"

"No problem!"

Seth looked over at her. "Sounds like he's commanding the troops."

"Yep. I apologize for telling you he was back there. I didn't stop to think it would distract you."

"I'm glad you told me." He put the truck in gear and drove away from the Burger Barn. "Now I'll recognize him. Sighting them one at a time is better than all at once."

"What if you run into several at the ranch?"

"It's a chance I have to take. Meeting Aunt Kendra is important and a ride is a great opportunity to get to know her a little. I'm counting on the others being either in town or up at the house."

"I hope you're right."

9

Seth ate his sandwich and fries without tasting either. He'd finished by the time Zoe directed him to turn off on the dirt road that led to the ranch. His heart rate picked up. His father could be at the end of that road.

Or not. Rory had created a brewing operation at the Guzzling Grizzly. Wouldn't he take his folks into town on their first day so he could show it off? That possibility calmed him somewhat.

Zoe drank the last of her lemonade and snapped on the lid. "Did you find the ranch site online?"

"Sure did." He crumbled his sandwich wrapper. "Can you please tuck this in the bag?"

"Sure." She added his trash to hers and rolled down the top of the bag before putting it on the floor. "If you went on the site, you must already know what the place looks like."

"I do."

"What did you think?"

"I'm particularly fond of the big ol' log ranch house." He stretched his arms against the steering wheel. "The rest of the place is nicely laid out and looks good, but log houses are my favorite. I had a Lincoln Logs set as a kid and ever since I've wanted to live in a house like that."

"It would fit you. Log houses have a rugged, manly appeal. I can see you building your own."

He smiled. "Because I'm so rugged and manly?"

"Now you're fishing."

"You're the one who threw me a line."

"Okay, yes, you're rugged and manly. Happy, now?"

"Yes, ma'am." Not really, but joking around allayed some of the anxiety churning in his stomach. He glanced at the clock on the dash. Aunt Kendra would be home by now.

"What else did you see on the website?"

"I found out they decorate the barn for Christmas."

"People do that?"

"Sure. I helped hang wreaths over the stall doors before I left. Had to use a ladder so we could put them out of reach or the horses will chew them to bits."

"Is that another thing you're good at? Decorating?"

"Come to think of it, I am."

"Me, too. I'm the one who put the red bows on the stair railings."

"Nice job." He drove around a curve and the ranch lay directly ahead. Braking slowly, he brought the truck to a stop, folded his arms over the steering wheel and gazed at the rambling log house. Smoke drifted from the chimney. "It looks even better than the pictures."

"I love the evergreen swags on the rail fence. And look at that wreath on the front door! It's twice as big as ours at the B&B."

"Big door." He pictured walking through it and shivered. Not today.

"It's massive, but you need a door like that. A typical one would look silly on that house." She glanced toward the barn. "Looks like Kendra's saddled our horses."

"And I hear a truck on the road behind us. Better get moving." He let up on the brake, stepped on the gas and drove toward the barn as a midnight blue truck rounded the turn. Likely he was related to the driver. Looked like only one person in the truck. That was a relief.

"Kendra's coming out of the barn."

"I see her." He parked the truck and shut off the motor. "A dyed-in-the-wool horsewoman."

"You can tell from here?"

"Sure can. It shows in the way she walks and moves. No question this is her domain." The knot in his chest loosened as he opened his door. He and Aunt Kendra would have common ground. "I look forward to meeting her."

Aunt Kendra came toward them. "Hey, Zoe! Good to see you."

"Same here. Aunt Mo said to say hello. And this is our guest Seth Turner."

Pulling off her work glove, she held out her hand. "Kendra McGavin."

He clasped her hand and held her gaze. Bryce had those same blue eyes. At first glance she looked too young to have five grown sons, but the wisdom in her eyes indicated a woman who'd triumphed over steep odds. "Pleased to meet you, ma'am."

"Same here, Seth." She surveyed him with open curiosity. "Have we met before?"

"No, ma'am."

"I feel like we have." She studied him more closely. "Actually, you remind me of my nephew Aleck. You two could be dopplegangers. You said you worked up near Glacier. Whereabouts?"

"Buckskin Ranch."

"I've heard good things about that place from some of my riders who've stayed there." Her manner was direct and approving, as if she'd sized him up and come to the same conclusion he had. They would get along. "I'm glad I could accommodate your request. It's been crazy around here."

"Holiday riders?"

"That, and my brother-in-law and his wife flew in from Scotland yesterday. I haven't seen Hamish since I was in high school and I'd never met Greer. We stayed up way too late last night."

Seth kept his expression neutral. "Easy to do when you reconnect after a long time." His stepmother's name was Greer. He tucked that information away.

"My nephews took them into town to have lunch at the Guzzling Grizzly. Have you been there, yet?"

"Zoe and I went there for dinner last night. Great spot. Enjoyed the McGavin's Pale Ale."

Her eyes shone with pride. "My nephew Rory is the brewer. I—" She glanced past them as a truck door slammed. "Excuse me, a minute. I need to check something with my son. Hey, Cody, did you get my message?"

"Yes, ma'am. Good thing I got there when I did. I bought the last three they had. They're in my truck."

"Awesome. Thank you." She returned her attention to Seth and Zoe. "Plush versions of Rudolph for the grandkids."

"They'll love 'em." Cody sauntered over. He shoved back his hat and held out his hand to Zoe. "Cody McGavin."

"Zoe Bradford."

"She's Maureen's niece," Aunt Kendra said.

"Oh, sure. Nice to finally meet you." He turned to Seth.

"Seth Turner." He clasped his cousin's hand. "Nice rig."

He smiled. "I'm partial to it, myself." His smile turned quizzical. "Have we met before? I feel as if I should know you."

"I told him the same thing," Aunt Kendra said. "I think it's because he looks a bit like Aleck."

"I can see that. Where are you from?"

"I work at the Buckskin Ranch."

"I've heard of it. I had a job at the Triangle V up in that same area."

"Ever go to the Choosy Moose Tavern?" What a kick if he and Cody had been there at the same time.

"No. I meant to check it out but never did." He shrugged. "I guess Mom's right. It's the resemblance to Aleck that has me thinking I know you. I wish he was here so you could meet each other." He glanced at Aunt Kendra. "When are they due back?"

"Around three." Aunt Kendra pulled her phone out of her coat pocket. "Speaking of that, we need to mount up."

"Yeah, I'd better get going, too." Cody checked his phone. "Faith's texting me about the plan for tomorrow night." He looked up. "Are you two going to the talent show?"

"We are," Zoe said.

"Then I'll see you both there. Mom, I'll take the Rudolphs up to the house and stick the bag in your bedroom."

"Thanks, son."

"Enjoy your ride. Nice meeting you, Seth. Zoe." He touched the brim of his hat and headed back toward his truck.

"Alrighty, then." Aunt Kendra gestured toward three horses lined up in front of the hitching post. "Zoe, you'll be on Strawberry, the roan in the middle. He's a true gentleman and everyone loves him. He's my go-to for anyone who has no experience with horses."

"Thanks. I appreciate that."

"Seth, I'm putting you on Jake, the big bay. He has some Tennessee Walker in him and he'll give you a very smooth ride. I'll take the lead on Licorice, that pretty little black mare, and you can bring up the rear on Jake."

He nodded. "Sounds good."

"Zoe and I will head into the barn and find her a hat. You're welcome to go over and make friends with Jake."

"Will do." He moved between the roan and the bay. Both geldings turned to gaze at him. "Hey, guys." He laid a hand on the silky neck of each one and soaked in their quiet strength.

Surrounded by their solid presence, he gradually relaxed. He needed horses in his life. Especially now. They anchored him like nothing else. He took a deep breath. "Nice place you've got, here."

Jake snorted and Strawberry bobbed his head.

"Looks like the McGavins take good care of you judging by the shine on your coats." He glanced down. "Hooves look healthy, too." He combed his fingers through Jake's mane. "No tangles. No burrs. Saddles are in good shape. I'd say you two have it made."

"Hey, Seth, are you sweet-talkin' my horses?"

He looked over his shoulder as Aunt Kendra approached. Zoe was behind her decked out in a Raptors Rise baseball cap. Adorable. He smiled. "Yes, ma'am, but neither of them will agree to go home with me."

"Guess I'm doing something right, then. Zoe, let me give you a hand up."

Seth continued to love on Jake while Aunt Kendra gave Zoe some basic instructions in an easy-going, yet confident, tone. No wonder the reviews left by happy riders had been so positive.

When Zoe said she was ready to go, he mounted up, put on his gloves and turned up his coat collar.

She glanced over at him with a bright smile. "I love this already and we haven't gone anywhere yet. Thanks for inviting me."

"I'm glad I did. Thought you'd take to it."

Aunt Kendra rode up beside him. "Stirrups good?"

"Perfect."

"My son Zane's the one who rides Jake the most and you're about the same height and build. He takes Jake for the raptor release trips."

"He does that on horseback?"

"Oh, yeah. That way he can release the birds in a more remote area. I've gone along several times. It's a thrill."

"I'll bet." One more thing on his growing list of experiences he'd love to have.

She turned back toward Zoe. "Follow me and call out if you have any problems."

"I doubt I will. Strawberry and I are already bonding."

Aunt Kendra grinned. "He loves the ladies. And we're off." She nudged the black mare forward.

Her evaluation of Jake's smooth gait was spot-on. A guy could take a snooze while riding the big bay and not be interrupted. But what man would want to snooze when he had Zoe Bradford riding ahead of him?

She was clearly having the time of her life, exclaiming over the unobstructed view as they rode out into a wide meadow. On the far side of it, snowcapped mountains, a blue sky and a few puffy clouds looked too beautiful to be real.

She'd lived in Eagles Nest for a month and likely had experienced some of the gorgeous scenery. But not from the back of a horse. He hadn't found any mode of transportation to equal it for total immersion in the environment. Her enthusiasm said plainly that she'd tapped into the joy of that experience.

He'd love to share more experiences like this with her. Take her up to Glacier and show her his favorite getaway spots. Except that wasn't realistic, was it? She was a mom-to-be who was leaving Montana in four months to raise her child alone. He had no place in that future.

But he could still dream.

10

When they came back from the ride a little past two, Cody had come back to the barn. He offered to unsaddle and groom the horses so his mother could go back to the house and take care of some Christmas-related tasks. Seth insisted on lending a hand. Zoe helped wherever she could, but this wasn't her skillset.

Clearly it was Seth's and Cody's. They worked together with an easy familiarity, swapping stories about the horses they'd dealt with over the years.

Seth was in high spirits as they drove away from the ranch. "What a beautiful ride, huh?"

"It was amazing. I didn't know what I'd been missing."

"Once you've seen the countryside from the back of a horse, nothing else compares."

"I know. Back in Wisconsin I've taken snowmobile runs with friends, but they're so noisy."

"Exactly. I've had to use one a time or two when I had to get somewhere in a hurry, but I'd rather be on a horse any day."

"So now you've met your aunt and another cousin."

"I have. And I don't know what I was worried about. These folks are just like me. They have more in the way of material goods, but they're horse people."

"Is it time for the big reveal, then?"

"If it weren't for my dad and his wife being here, I'd have told Aunt Kendra today. But she was up late last night and so was my dad. I don't think it's nice to hit folks with an emotional issue when they're exhausted."

"Maybe tomorrow, then?"

"That's my current thinking. In the meantime, I want to see Raptors Rise. And meet Zane, if he's around."

"There's a work of art in the lobby that everyone talks about. I'm eager to see that, too."

"Home Sweet Home?"

"So you know about it?"

"It's featured on the Raptors Rise website. I liked it so much I did some research on Quinn Sawyer and his scratchboard art. I plan to buy a print of it before I leave."

"Do you know that he and Kendra are together?"

"No, I didn't."

"They are, although Quinn keeps his own place on the other side of the main road."

"Interesting. They're not married?"

"Not as far as I know, but Aunt Mo says they're devoted to each other."

"I can't imagine living across the road from the woman I love."

"Aunt Mo thinks it's because they were both single for so many years. His wife died young, just like your Uncle Ian. They could be set in their ways."

"That might be why I haven't made an effort to move out of the bunkhouse. Keeps me flexible. If I had my own place, I could get set in my ways, too." He slowed the truck and pulled into the parking area in front of the Raptors Rise visitor center. "My mom did."

"She didn't date?"

"Nope." He circled the lot and found a spot. "I asked her about it once when I was old enough to think about such things. I wondered if it was because of me. She said she just had no interest in dating." He shut off the engine but made no move to get out.

Neither did she. This conversation might be the first one he'd ever had on the subject. "So why didn't she have an interest?"

"I think she was a one-man woman. But despite that, she couldn't imagine giving up Montana to live in Scotland and my dad loved Scotland and wanted to go back. They were at an impasse."

"That's sad. Maybe it really was too painful for her to talk about."

"Maybe. I look a lot like him, so I must have been a constant reminder that she'd given up the love of her life. I can't fault her for wanting to stay in Montana. I'm firmly planted here, too. But I wish she'd told me who my dad was."

"What was her name?"

"Helen Marie."

"Pretty name."

"Pretty lady. I hope he remembers her. It would suck if he doesn't. But that's for another day." He reached for his door handle. "Let's go see some eagles."

"Okay."

The place was packed. After buying tickets for the next available tour, Seth bought her a Raptors Rise cap. "You need this," he said as he handed it to her. "You looked so cute in it during the ride. If you go again, you won't have to borrow one from Aunt Kendra."

She couldn't refuse such a sweet gesture, although she couldn't see herself spending money on horseback rides when she was squirreling money away for baby expenses. "Thank you." She adjusted the fit and put it on.

His gaze warmed. "Very nice."

She basked in that warmth for as long as she dared before looking away. "Let's check out *Home Sweet Home.*"

"Sure thing."

They joined the crowd gathered in front of a life-sized image of an eagle's nest with chicks in the nest and the parents standing guard on the perimeter.

Zoe waited as people in the front drifted away. Then she moved closer. "Spectacular."

"I might have to get a bigger print than I planned on. A small one won't do it justice."

"You said you researched Quinn's scratchboard art. Did you find out how he creates this 3-D effect?"

"As I understand it, he starts with a board covered with white clay and black ink. He scratches out the image and sometimes, like in this case, he adds color."

"The detail is incredible. Any minute I expect one of those adult eagles to fly away."

"No kidding. The feathers look real. Now I'm thinking I want an actual scratchboard he's done. I won't be satisfied with a print. No texture."

"Could be pricey."

"I'm sure. On top of that, I don't have a place to hang it."

"The disadvantage of living in a bunkhouse, I guess."

"Yeah, and I'm determined to take something of his home with me, which is not my usual M.O. I never had the urge to buy wall art before."

She glanced at him. "You may be outgrowing the bunkhouse."

"Could be. What was that your aunt said about the nesting instinct?"

She smiled. "That this town brings it out in people."

"I'll bet the urge to buy wall art is one of the symptoms. Although I'd be dumb to do it, I don't think I can help myself. I—"

"Tour Six! If you're holding a ticket for Tour Six, meet me to the right of the counter, please!"

She turned toward the speaker and read the name embroidered on the front of his jacket. "Guess what? We get Zane as our tour guide. With a baby carrier strapped to his manly chest."

"His baby?"

"I think so. I'm fairly certain Aunt Mo said Zane and his wife had a little boy and that baby's hair is black like Zane's." She lowered her voice. "That looks like baby food on the collar of Zane's shirt, so yeah, it's likely his child. Oh, my God, look at the kid's feet sticking out of the carrier. He's wearing tiny cowboy boots."

"I didn't know they made them that small."

"They make all kinds of cool stuff for babies. I'll have to watch myself or I'll blow through my budget."

Group Six gathered around Zane. Zoe counted ten visitors, including her and Seth.

Zane cleared his voice. "Welcome to Raptors Rise, folks. I'm Zane McGavin and this little guy is my son Rhys. Yes, we're both wearing his lunch. Didn't have time to clean up."

"Ga!" The baby reached up and patted his chin.

His dad caught his hand and held onto it. "Our mission at Raptors Rise is to rehabilitate injured birds and release them whenever possible. If they would be unsafe in the wild, we keep them safe here. If they can fly, we exercise them daily in our flight enclosure."

"Ga!" The baby bounced in his carrier and Zane laid a restraining hand on his small shoulder.

A young girl raised her hand. "Can we touch the birds?"

"Good question. It's better for them if we have as little contact as possible so they don't become used to humans. When we visit the enclosures, please stay behind the ropes and keep your voices down. These are wild creatures and we want to keep it that way. Any other questions before we start?"

"How old is Rhys?" someone called out.

Zane beamed. "Six months plus. He was born on July second. Any other questions?" He glanced around. "Okay, we'll begin with the Badger Calhoun Nursery. Badger's a good friend to Raptors Rise so we named the nursery in his honor."

Seth leaned toward Zoe. "Is Badger the one your aunt called a force of nature?"

"Yep." She filed past the nursery door and took her turn at peeking in. "He and Ryker co-own Badger Air."

"A man of many skills."

"He's not shy about telling you that, either. He stops by the B&B all the time to give Aunt Mo a hug. She helped him win over Hayley. Their wedding took place before I got here and evidently it was amazing. Badger played the bagpipes during the ceremony."

"Huh." Seth grinned. "Can't wait to meet the guy."

Zane turned toward the group. "Now we'll head outside. Bundle up, folks. It's chilly out there." Before he opened the door, he pulled a knit hat out of his jacket pocket and put it on Rhys. Rhys pulled the hat off and Zane put it back on.

Rhys yanked it off again. Zane grabbed it before it fell to the floor and leaned toward his child, murmuring something. This time when he put on the hat, Rhys left it alone. When his dad opened the door and started down the path toward the large wood and wire enclosures, Rhys bounced in his carrier and made cooing sounds.

"Your kid sounds excited about the birds," a guy said.

"He loves them. Come back in a few years and he'll be leading tours." Zane paused and faced the group. "We'll start with the hawks, move on to the owls and finish with the eagles. You're welcome to take pictures, but please mute your phones."

Zoe silenced her phone but kept it handy. "I'm going to send pictures to my mom and dad," she murmured. "They visited Aunt Mo two years ago and came here, but I know the operation's expanded a lot since then. They'll love seeing how it's flourishing."

"I'm going to spread the word, too." Seth pulled out his phone. "Some of my buddies would love this and when the weather's nice, it's only a day trip."

"How many hours?"

"Should be less than four, but yesterday the snow turned it into more like seven." He glanced at her. "I'm still taking it one day at a time, but if everything keeps going this well…"

"You'll be driving down regularly to visit your family?"

"Maybe not just them."

Uh-oh. A little flirtation was one thing. Containable.

"Unless you wouldn't want me to see you."

"Uh—"

"We can talk about it later." He gestured toward the first enclosure. "That red-tailed hawk is posing for you."

"So it is. Thanks."

For the rest of the tour she gave her attention to the majestic birds and Zane's commentary. She snapped a ton of pictures. Sending the best of the bunch to her parents would be a nice pre-Christmas gift.

They'd planned to visit in April when her baby was due, but they'd also talked about flying out before then for a long weekend, maybe in January. This might nudge them to make the extra trek.

But she wouldn't be introducing them to Seth, would she? How had she missed the implications of Seth connecting with his family? Naturally he'd want to strengthen the relationship by coming back again soon. And often.

As they ended the tour and started back to the visitor center, Seth touched her arm. "I'd like to speak to Zane for a minute before we leave."

"Me, too. He's done an incredible job with the sanctuary."

"Makes me proud to know I'm related to him."

She smiled. "That's awesome."

"Yeah, like you said, this is a great bunch of people. Now I wish I'd read the diary right after I found it." He held the door for her as they walked back into the visitor center.

"I can see why you held off. You knew it would be an emotional experience."

"Didn't know just how emotional. Or life-changing." He glanced at the group that had gathered around Zane. "We can wait until the others are done."

"Fine with me."

"You know, maybe I read the diary at exactly the right time. If I'd come here last Christmas, you'd have been in Milwaukee."

"And dating my ex, who didn't have much use for Christmas."

Seth opened his mouth, then closed it again and shook his head.

"I know. I should have questioned that, too. All my focus was on my yoga studio and I didn't give much thought to how crappy my relationship was."

"I've never seriously considered being my own boss, but I can see the appeal of having more control over your destiny."

"I always knew that was what I wanted. Hey, the last people are leaving. Let's grab him." She hurried over to Zane. "That was wonderful. I'm Zoe, by the way, Maureen Stanislowski's niece."

He smiled. "I kind of thought that was you. Glad you liked it. And brought a friend."

"This is Seth Turner. He's staying at the B&B for the holidays."

Seth shook his hand. "Good meeting you, Zane. What a fantastic project you have going here."

"Thanks. It's dear to my heart. And Mandy's. We talked about it when we were kids and now it's a reality."

Zoe peered at Rhys. "Somebody's fast asleep."

"I'm not surprised. It's his nap time."

"I'm curious about what you said to him that made him stop taking off his hat."

"I told him if he didn't leave it on, he wouldn't get to see the birds. That did the trick. He doesn't talk yet, but he understands a heck of a lot."

"How would you have kept him from seeing the birds? You were leading a tour."

He gave her a sheepish grin. "I was bluffing. Fortunately, he's not old enough to figure that out. I'm on duty today while Mandy finishes up some costumes for the talent show. Are either of you going?"

"Aunt Mo got us tickets a while ago and picked up one for Seth today. Are you performing?"

"I am. And you'll have to forgive me for that." He gazed at Seth. "You sure do remind me of my cousin Aleck. And my Uncle Hamish, come to think of it."

"I've been told that."

"He brought his bagpipes from Scotland, if you can believe it. He'll be playing with his two sons and Badger Calhoun, the guy we named our nursery after. It should be quite the show-stopper."

But not as big a show-stopper as the news Seth would soon be delivering to the McGavin clan. She hoped it went well, for all their sakes.

<u>11</u>

"It's time for me to set up a meeting with Aunt Kendra, my dad and his wife," Seth announced as he drove away from Raptors Rise. Instead of dreading the encounter, he was eager to get it out of the way and move on.

"All three instead of just Kendra?"

"No reason to take it in stages. After meeting Aunt Kendra, I'm confident she can handle it. No telling how my dad and his wife will react. But they can break the news to my half-brothers."

"And Kendra can inform her sons?"

"That's my thought. I think that'll go fine. I've met three and eyeballed one. But Aunt Kendra mentioned during the ride that she had five sons. Who am I missing?"

"Trevor. He works for a local construction company plus does jobs on the side. Aunt Mo hired him to replace some loose shingles this fall, and he's been back to do small repairs a couple of times since, which is when I met him."

"What's he like?"

She smiled. "He's a fun guy. He can sing, too. I was cleaning the third-floor room while he was working outside. He was belting out *Boot Scootin' Boogie.*"

"Do you think he'll be in the talent show?"

"I think all the McGavins will be in the talent show."

"Even Ryker? Somehow I can't picture him—"

"He juggles."

"No way. What does he juggle?"

"Christmas plates. Aunt Mo said he's done it the past two years."

"I'll be damned." He sighed. "Sounds great."

"Juggling?"

"All of it."

"It will be. When do you plan to go out to the ranch?"

"The sooner the better. I'd love to talk with them tonight, but like I said before, they all must be running on fumes by now."

"Speaking of running on fumes…"

He glanced over. "Tired?"

"I blame it on the baby. My stamina isn't what it was five months ago."

"Then what do you say we head to the diner, eat early and drive back to the B&B?"

"That sounds fabulous. Thank you."

"My pleasure." He stopped at the main road, waited for traffic to clear and made a left towards town.

"If you've ruled out going to the ranch tonight, when would you like to?"

"Tomorrow morning if Aunt Kendra agrees. I want this out in the open before the talent show."

"Good call."

"After we get settled at the diner I'll contact her. It'll be disruptive whenever I go, but it needs to happen."

"I agree."

He glanced to his right as they approached the Guzzling Grizzly. "The GG is hopping again tonight." He was proud of himself for using the initials instead of the name. Made him sound like a local.

"If you slow down, I can check for the Wild Creek van." She searched the parking lot. "Uh-huh. There it is."

"I guess I'll text Aunt Kendra instead of trying to call her. I hope she sees it."

"All you can do is try. Okay, you're coming up on the diner."

"Thanks." He pulled into the parking lot and found a spot. "Looks like we beat the crowd."

"This was a good move. It'll be busy later on. Evidently Eagles Nest gets more popular every year."

"Since there's no hotel, where do they all stay?"

"The Crimson Clouds guest ranch opened for the Christmas season this year. When Aunt Mo was booked solid, she sent people over there. Some out-of-towners probably have relatives here and stay with them, like your dad and his wife."

"Your aunt told me when I booked my room that I got the last one."

"And that was because of a cancellation. Otherwise you might have ended up at the Crimson Clouds."

"And wouldn't have met you."

"Probably not."

He gazed at her in the soft glow of twilight. "That's hard to imagine." Leaning over to give her a gentle kiss would be so easy. Instead he unsnapped his seatbelt. "Better get inside before the rush."

The diner was fairly empty, but it radiated Christmas cheer. A hand-painted mural of the North Pole decorated the windows and carols greeted him as he opened the door. Mouthwatering aromas reminded his stomach that he was hungry, too.

A hostess wearing a Christmas-themed vest met them as soon as they stepped inside. "Welcome to the Eagles Nest Diner. Table, booth or counter?"

Seth glanced at Zoe. "Your choice. I picked last night."

"A booth, please."

"Perfect. Follow me." She led them to a booth, laid down two menus and promised a server would be along shortly.

Lights twinkled in a garland draped along the windowsill, and snowflakes dangled from the ceiling. He glanced around. "Festive."

After he helped Zoe out of her parka, she settled into her side of the cushy booth with a sigh. "Thank you for bringing me here. I'm in the mood for low-key ambiance and comfort food."

"What qualifies as comfort food?" He took off his jacket and laid it along with her parka on his side before sliding in and picking up the menu.

"Meatloaf, mashed potatoes and homemade gravy. Some tasty steamed veggie like carrots or green beans, but no salad. I don't want to work too hard."

"My mom was a whiz at meatloaf."

"You said she was the ranch cook?"

He nodded. "Making food for hungry ranch hands gave her pleasure. She'd been disappointed in love, but she doted on me and basked in the praise of those cowboys."

"And never found that special guy among them?"

"I never saw her flirt. Once in a while someone would try to engage her on that level, but she refused to play. She treated them as good friends and nothing more."

"Are you going to tell your dad any of this?"

"No. She wouldn't have wanted me to."

Her expression softened. "And it's sweet that you're honoring her wishes."

"Which means I can't let him read her diary."

"That's right, but you could take the pictures out and let him see those. I doubt it will be necessary to prove yourself. As everyone keeps saying, you look like a member of the family. Speaking of that, what about Kendra?"

"I'll wait until after we order. And here comes our server. What do you want to drink?"

"Hot chocolate with whipped cream, please."

He laughed. "The ultimate comfort drink." Turning to the woman approaching the table, he asked for two identical orders.

After she left, Zoe rolled her eyes. "You don't have to keep giving the same order as me."

"I really wanted the meatloaf. You have to work at eating fried chicken." He pulled out his phone and scrolled through his contacts. "You know what? I don't have her cell number, just the ranch land line."

"Let me text Aunt Mo. She'll have it." She pulled out her phone and sent a message. Then she glanced up. "She's texting Kendra to ask her to contact you."

"Which is the right way to do it. Good for her that she doesn't freely give out cell numbers."

"She's discreet. She's kept my secret about the baby. I need to let her know it's okay to say something, now. I'll give her the line I plan to use with people so she can use it, too."

Another reminder that she planned to raise her kid alone. No dad in the picture. Sounded so lonely.

His phone pinged, distracting him. "That could be Aunt Kendra." He checked the screen. "It's her. Excuse me a minute."

"No worries."

He quickly typed in the request he'd come up with. *I had a great time at the ranch today. Would've liked to stay longer, see the whole operation. Could I come out first thing in the* morning and help feed? After he sent the message, he turned his phone around so Zoe could read it.

She nodded. "Good plan."

The reply came right back. Sure. Always happy to show off my stable. Be here at seven.

Thanks! See you then. He hit Send. "Game on."

"Congratulations."

"I'll tell her and then let her decide how to handle it with my dad."

"And her family."

"Yep." He dragged in a breath and leaned back against the booth. "Damn, this is hard."

"You'll be fine."

"Like I said today, I hope he remembers my mom."

"He might remember and downplay the relationship because his wife is there. Be sure and show him the pictures. Helen Marie needs to be acknowledged. She's the mother of his son."

"Damn straight." He tucked his phone away. "Once I tell Aunt Kendra, I wonder who she'll want to bring on the scene."

"Her sons, the women in their lives, your half-brothers and their sweethearts."

"It'll be a circus."

"And you'll be the ringmaster."

He exhaled. "But I don't want—"

"To be surrounded by a bunch of relatives? Seth, you're working toward a crowded Thanksgiving table. You need lots of folks to make that happen."

He held her gaze. "I suppose I do. Full steam ahead."

"That's the spirit. It's the goal you had when you arrived. Now you'll make it happen."

He smiled. "Create a plan and follow the plan."

"It works."

"But sometimes you come across the unexpected."

"Like your dad and stepmom?"

"Like them. And you. I couldn't have predicted that my landlady would have a niece I'd... like very much."

Her expression softened. "I like you very much, too."

"I threw you for a loop when I mentioned coming back for visits." His chest tightened, but he wanted to know where he stood.

"Well, I—" She glanced up. "Here comes our food."

He'd wait, but he wasn't going to drop the subject. The server placed two steaming plates in front of them, along with whipped-cream topped mugs of hot chocolate. "Looks delicious."

"Doesn't it?" Zoe unwrapped her silverware from the cloth napkin. "This baby has really increased my appetite."

She'd mentioned another unsatisfied appetite during last night's conversation... nope, not going there. "I guess that *eating for two* business is true, then." He laid his napkin in his lap and picked up his fork.

"Sure is in my case." She cradled her hot chocolate in both hands and took a sip. Got some whipped cream on her upper lip. Licked it away.

When his groin tightened, he focused on eating until the tension eased. *Get it together, Turner.* Why now? He'd made it through several hours without this inconvenient reaction. Several hours of constant activity, though.

Now they were face-to-face, separated only by less than three feet of tabletop. Good thing they weren't at the GG, because he'd ask her to dance. It would be torture, but he'd welcome any opportunity to hold her in his arms again.

Create a plan. Follow the plan. He put down his fork. "Let's say that you're right, and the McGavins are happy to welcome me into the family."

"I think that's a safe assumption."

"So do I, at least for Aunt Kendra and my cousins. Which means I'll come back to see them whenever possible. You'll still be here. What's the plan?"

She made eye contact and then looked away. "I've been thinking about that."

"I figured."

She lifted her gaze to his. "The bottom line is that I'm going back to Milwaukee in April."

If he'd wanted a flicker of uncertainty, he wasn't going to get it. Disappointment settled in his gut. "Given that, what do you want to do?"

"The question is what do *you* want to do, knowing I'll be leaving? Knowing that each time you come to town, I'll be more pregnant? You might discover you're not so—"

"No, I won't discover that. If you're here, I want to see you. That's my bottom line. If you're okay with that, I'd like to plan that we'll get together whenever I'm in town."

She took a shaky breath. "Then that's our plan."

"Good." It was way better than nothing.

12

The Nesting Place parking area was deserted. Happy Hour was over and the guests had all driven into town for dinner.

Seth parked the truck. "Wait for me to help you out. It's slippery."

She waited. Never mind that she'd been dealing with ice and snow her entire life. His gallant behavior was charming. And arousing. She'd been fighting her pesky hormones all day.

As a beginning rider, she hadn't dared take pictures of him mounted on that magnificent horse, but she had a boatload of mental pictures of his muscled thighs gripping the horse's belly and his capable hands on the reins. She was a little sorry he hadn't galloped out into that meadow.

But that wasn't Seth. Not even slightly a showoff.

Then, over dinner, he'd laid his cards on the table. The warmth in his eyes when he'd announced his bottom line—keeping the connection no matter what—had created a firestorm of needs that wouldn't be fulfilled. Dammit.

He helped her down and kept a firm grip on her arm as he navigated the narrow path through the packed snow in the parking lot. He didn't let go until she was standing on the porch. She didn't want him to let go at all.

Aunt Mo was at her desk typing away at her computer when they walked in. She glanced up and smiled. "There you two are. Did you have a good day?"

Zoe unzipped her parka. "We sure did. The ride was amazing and then we went to Raptors Rise."

"Wonderful!"

"It just blows me away. The birds are gorgeous, and when I think of what would have happened to each of them without Zane's efforts..." She shuddered.

"I know. Did he tell you he wants to open another sanctuary somewhere else in the state?"

"I don't think so." Slipping out of her parka, she turned to Seth. "Did you hear anything about that?"

"Sure didn't." He finished unbuttoning his jacket. "Any idea where he might locate it?"

"Last I heard, he was still researching the best spot."

"Then I'd like to talk to him. Apple Grove might be exactly what he's looking for. Have you ever been there?"

She shook her head. "You're the first person I've met who's from that town."

"It's small, about the size of Eagles Nest, and we're near Glacier, so the sanctuary would get foot traffic. I can pretty much guarantee local support. Several of my buddies would volunteer, and I sure would."

"Then mention that to Zane next time you see him. I guess that might be tomorrow night."

"Might be."

Her aunt shut down the computer. "I was about to have my evening cup of tea. Anyone care to join me?"

Evening tea had been a nightly ritual before Seth had arrived yesterday. A calming cup of tea was exactly what she needed. "I'd love that, Aunt Mo." She hung up her parka.

Seth hesitated. "Thank you for the invitation, but I'm not much of a tea drinker."

"I could pour you something stronger."

"Thank you, ma'am, but I think I'll just mosey on up to my room."

Zoe turned to him. "Thanks for a great day."

"My pleasure." He held her gaze. "See you in the morning."

"Oh, but—" She caught herself before she blurted out something she shouldn't.

"I'll come down a little early."

"All right. See you then."

"Have a good night, ladies." He crossed the room quickly and took the stairs two at a time.

"What a sweet man," Aunt Mo murmured softly.

"Uh-huh."

Her aunt lifted her eyebrows. "Aha."

"Let's go have some tea."

"And conversation?"

Zoe laughed as she headed back to Aunt Mo's private quarters and into her small kitchen. "Nothing to talk about." She filled the electric kettle, plugged it in and flipped the switch.

"So you say. That man is good for you, Zoe."

"He is?"

"Absolutely." She took a canister of tea from a cupboard. "You look happier than you've been since you arrived."

"Hey, wait, I haven't been un—"

"I know, and you've told me a million times how much you enjoy it here. But when you walked through that door tonight, your eyes were sparkling." She got out a teapot and measured the tea into it.

"No wonder." Zoe chose two flowered teacups and saucers from Aunt Mo's private collection and took them into the adjacent sitting room. "The ride was incredible and I can't stop thinking about the raptor center."

"Or Seth?" Her aunt brought in the teapot and a trivet.

Zoe sighed. "It's a non-starter. I'm not exactly free to date." She placed a hand on her belly. "And besides, I'm leaving in April."

"I suppose." She ducked back into the kitchen and returned with a jar of honey and a couple of spoons. After ladling honey into each cup, she settled into her favorite chair.

Zoe took the one on the other side of the lace-covered tea table. "It might be easier if his room wasn't right next to mine."

"Maybe." Aunt Mo poured the tea. "He's definitely interested in you."

"I know. I've explained that my hormones are going crazy because of the pregnancy, but—"

"You told him that?" Aunt Mo chuckled. "When?"

"On the way home from the GG last night. We danced a couple of times and both of us were a little worked up. I emphasized that I had a hormonal issue and he assured me he had no intention of doing... anything."

"Because he's an honorable man."

"And I'm an honorable mom-to-be, so I won't be taking advantage of his interest in me." She picked up her tea and began sipping it slowly.

"Not even if he wants you to?"

She choked on her tea. Setting the cup and saucer on the table, she cleared her throat and stared at her aunt. "What?"

"I've seen the way he looks at you. In my experience, most men will gladly take a little bit of sex over no sex."

Zoe's eyes widened. "Are you saying I should—"

"Ask him? Maybe. He's a good man and you're consenting adults. I assume you've been clear that you're leaving town after the baby's born?"

"I've been extremely clear that I'm leaving."

"There you go. He's visiting, too. You're just taking advantage of an opportunity to make each other happy for a little while." She took another drink of her tea. "You even have connecting doors. Nobody has to be the wiser."

Zoe's cheeks warmed, but so did the rest of her. "I'll have to state it that way. That I'm only talking about a temporary arrangement. He might not go for it."

"There's always that chance. I'd say it's about as likely as me doing a striptease for the talent show, but you have to be okay with it if he turns you down."

"He could be asleep."

"At eight-thirty?"

She took a shaky breath. "I'll go ask him."

13

Propped in bed reading a paperback Western he'd brought on the trip, Seth waited for the sound of Zoe's footsteps on the stairs. Once she'd gone back to her room, he'd head down and get some cookies.

He should have grabbed some before coming up here. Aunt Mo kept a bottomless cookie jar on the hutch in the breakfast room. But he'd been too intent on getting away from Zoe and her tempting mouth.

Maybe she was giving off pheromones. Or maybe he'd reached the limit of his sexual self-control. In any case, kissing her full mouth had become an obsession during the remainder of their dinner. Every bite she'd taken had sent him closer to the edge.

Driving the truck had created a distraction, but once they were back in the B&B in full light, he'd zeroed in again. He'd taken himself out of the line of fire, but now he craved cookies. They wouldn't be much of a substitute, but they'd have to do.

Ah, there it was, her boots on the stairs, topping the landing. Evidently she hadn't worried about waking him. Good guess on her part. Considering what he had coming up in the morning, he might not sleep much at all.

Sticking a slip of paper in the book, he closed it and laid it on the nightstand. Then he swung his legs off the bed and stood. He'd left on his jeans and t-shirt for the cookie raid. Once her door opened and closed, he'd be on his way. No reason to put on his boots.

Here she came. Then her steps slowed. She was stopping *here*? If she wanted to have a conversation, he was so screwed. He could refuse to open the door. Nah, he couldn't do that.

She tapped on it. "Seth?"

He braced himself and opened the door. Oh, God. He clenched his fists so he wouldn't pull her into the room and kiss her until... forever. "What's up?"

"Listen, I've been thinking." She twisted her fingers together like people did when they were nervous.

"About what?"

"Could I come in? I'd like to talk about something."

No! If you come into my bedroom, I can't be responsible for what happens. "Sure." He stepped aside to let her in. Her color was high. Something was bugging the hell out of her.

She sucked in a breath. "This is awkward."

"Does it have something to do with Aunt Mo?" She hadn't communicated with anyone else so far as he knew.

"Not really. Well, I suppose it does, in a way."

Her twisting fingers made him crazy. He covered her hands with his. "Zoe, what is it?"

She lifted her gaze to his. "I confided in her that you... turn me on."

He gulped. "And she said..."

"That I should ask you if you want to have temporary sex because maybe some sex is better than no sex and we're two consenting adults and why shouldn't we just enjoy ourselves?" She paused to take a breath. "If you want to. You might not, because I really am leaving and so there's—"

"You're kidding, right?" His heart hammered and breathing became a chore.

Her response was almost a whisper. "No. Not kidding."

"Zoe, I would crawl over broken glass to spend even one night with you."

"You would? Even though this can't go anywhere?"

"Even then. Are you saying you want that? You want me to make love to you?"

She swallowed. "Yes, please."

He squeezed her hands and let go. "Then I'd better close the door." His hand shook as he pushed it shut and twisted the lock. "You caught me unprepared." He turned back to her. "I don't have any—"

"I didn't expect you to. I thought about that on the way up here."

He couldn't help smiling. "Do you have a plan?"

She nodded. "I'm pregnant, so I've been tested for everything. I'm fine. But if you have issues, then we can—"

"I'm clear, too. I haven't been with anyone since before my mother died. But you only have my word on any of that."

"If I couldn't trust you, I wouldn't be here."

"Fair enough." He approached her slowly. Framing her face in both hands, he gazed into her eyes. Then he kissed her gently, tasting, absorbing the texture of her velvet mouth. He drew back, his voice husky. "I keep thinking this can't be real. I told myself it couldn't happen."

"Me, too." She slid her palms up his chest and gripped his shoulders. "And it's just for now. When you come back, I'll be—"

"Shh." He feathered kisses over her forehead, her cheeks, her chin. "Let's not worry about that. Let's just love each other now."

She let out a slow breath. "That sounds lovely."

"It will be. I promise you it will be." Leaning down, he nuzzled the curve of her throat. "You didn't take off your boots before climbing the stairs."

She arched her neck to give him greater access. "I thought about it."

He chuckled. "Why didn't you?" God, she smelled delicious and tasted even better. He buried his fingers in her curls and tilted her head so he could nibble her earlobe.

"Because I knew you weren't sleeping and nobody else is here so there was no reason to take them off unless I expected to have sex with you and if you said no I'd be standing there with my boots in my hand, looking foolish." She sucked in a breath. "That's why."

He gazed into her beautiful brown eyes. "You seriously thought I'd say no?"

"If it bothered you that there were limits."

"Oh, it bothers me. It doesn't stop me."

She frowned. "If it bothers you, then—"

"Hear me, Zoe. I'm crazy about you. Would I rather have the possibility of a future with you? Damn right I would. But if I can't, then I'll take what I can get. Starting now." He captured her mouth and took the kiss deep. If this was all he could have, he'd make it count.

She caught fire, opening to him, digging her fingers into his shoulders, pressing her sweet body against his.

He guided her back to the bed and lifted his mouth from hers. "Boots first."

She sat on the edge of the mattress and he broke the kiss long enough to kneel before her, tug off her boots and toss them aside. On his knees turned out to be the perfect position for grasping the hem of her shirt and pulling it over her head. While he was at it, he reached behind her back and unhooked her bra.

Her breasts spilled out in all their glory.

"Wow."

"They're bigger than usual, since..."

"Can I touch you?"

"Sure."

"Will it hurt?"

"It doesn't when I touch them. It just feels good."

"I've never...you look so...ripe." He cradled a breast in each hand. "You feel that way, too."

"You can squeeze them. I like that sensation."

His fingers flexed. "Me, too." His breath caught as liquid dribbled out. "Is that milk?"

"The precursor to milk."

He licked his lips. "Can I...?"

"Yes."

Leaning closer, he lapped gently with his tongue. "It's sweet."

"I know."

He glanced up through his thick lashes. "You've tasted it?"

"Of course. Why wouldn't I?"

"And why wouldn't I?" His attention returned to her breasts. At first he only licked. Then he began to suck.

She gripped his biceps. "Seth..."

He paused, raised his head. "Am I hurting you?"

"You're going to make me come."

His gaze darkened. "You should be more comfy when that happens." Releasing her breasts, he grasped the waistband of her jeans. "We need to get rid of all this."

She smiled. "If you say so."

He stripped off her jeans and panties in record time, scooped her up and laid her on the bed. "Might as well get rid of the rest of mine while I'm at it." He ditched his t-shirt with one swift tug and got rid of his jeans, briefs and socks almost as fast.

She held out her hand. "Will you let me touch you?"

"A little bit." He stepped closer. "I'm not in complete control right now."

"I can tell." She swiped a thumb over the glistening drop at the tip of his cock. Then she sucked her thumb.

He groaned. "Should have seen that coming."

"If you'll join me, we'll both be coming in no time." She opened her arms. "Make love to me, Seth."

"As if I could help it." He put a knee on the mattress and carefully moved over her, settling gently between her thighs. "As if I haven't been thinking of this since the first moment I saw you."

"Shoveling snow?" She stroked his back and he quivered beneath her touch.

"Uh-huh."

"What's..." She gulped as he probed her entrance with the blunt tip of his cock. "What's... sexy about that?"

He held her gaze. "Everything you do is sexy." He eased forward and paused. "You're so alive."

"I sure am feeling alive right now."

"You'd better coach me."

"Coach you?"

"I've never made love to a pregnant lady."

"I've been told I can do anything I feel like doing."

Heat coursed through his veins. "But let's be careful this first time."

"Okay." Sliding her hands down to grip his firm butt, she lifted her hips, taking him deeper. "How's that?"

His voice rasped in the quiet room. "Incredible." A twinge warned him she was close.

"You might as well... finish the job."

"I will." His jaw tightened as he sank slowly into her channel. "But if it's too much..." Gentle contractions followed the slide of his cock. This was going to be good. And soon.

She gasped out his name.

He froze. "Did I hurt—"

"*No.*" She dug her fingertips into his glutes. "I'm gonna come. Cover my mouth."

With a sharp intake of breath, he cupped his hand over her mouth and pushed home.

She erupted, her strangled cry muffled as she arched into him and surrendered to her climax.

He stayed immobile, his breathing ragged, until she stopped moaning. Then he took his hand away. "You all right?"

She gazed up at him and dragged in air. "Never better. That was awesome."

"Good."

"But you haven't—"

"Not yet. But I will." He lifted away and his gaze swept over her. "You're pink all over."

"Because I'm happy all over."

"And beautiful all over."

"Aww."

"Think I'll hang out up here for a while so I can look at you while I do this." Hovering over her, balanced on his outstretched arms, he initiated a relaxed rhythm. "Maybe you'll come again."

"I just might."

"That's all I need to hear." He shifted the angle so he pressed more firmly on her trigger point. "How's that?"

She sucked in a breath. "Great."

"Faster?"

"Yes, please."

He picked up the pace.

She pressed her hands against the bed to give herself the leverage to match him thrust for thrust. "Come with me."

His chest heaved. "I intend to."

Holding his gaze, he drew closer and closer to his release. Her body echoed the excitement rising in his. Faster. And faster yet.

He gulped in air. "Can you?"

She nodded as the spring tightened one more notch.

He tensed. "*Now.*"

"Yes."

He plunged deep and clenched his jaw, his body shuddering.

Her orgasm flowed over and around his. Following his lead, she swallowed her cries as the tremors rolled through her.

He maintained his position and gasped for breath, but gradually the gasping gave way to soft laughter. "That... was so... good." He shook his head in disbelief. Then he looked down at her. "Is it just me, or are we spectacular together?"

"It's not just you." She smiled up at him. "We rock."

<u>14</u>

Thank you, Aunt Mo. Zoe lay cuddled in Seth's arms, her cheek resting against his muscled shoulder.

He pulled her closer. "And here I was wondering how I'd get through the night."

"So why didn't you take Aunt Mo's offer of a nightcap?"

"Because all I could think about was how much I wanted to kiss you."

She glanced up in surprise. "That's why you took off so fast?"

"Uh-huh." He brushed his thumb over her lower lip. "Watching you lick whipped cream off your mouth started me down that road and I couldn't seem to find an off-ramp."

"I had no idea."

"I didn't want to let on." He traced the bow of her upper lip. "Remember when you buttered a dinner roll and got melted butter on your fingers?"

"I guess so."

"You licked that off, too. Thank God the table hid my reaction."

"I didn't mean to torture you."

"I know." He smiled. "Doesn't matter now. You're here."

"Feeling better?"

"Much better." He tilted her chin up. "But your mouth still drives me crazy."

"I like crazy."

"That's good news." Leaning down, he kissed her.

And the magic was back. With Seth, making love wasn't just an idle phrase. He was all in. Tender caresses from his work-roughened hands created an all-consuming need that only he could satisfy. When he thrust deep, she gasped, dazzled by the power of their intense connection.

His gaze locked with hers as he slowly began to move. Boundaries dissolved. She surrendered gladly to this moment, to this man. Gradually he coaxed her to the brink.

"Now." His soft murmur was followed by one more vigorous stroke that swept her into a whirlpool of joy. Beautiful.

She clung to him as he found his own release, throwing back his head, his breath hissing through his teeth. As he shuddered in her arms, tension drained from his muscular body.

She stroked his sweaty back and urged him to give her his full weight.

"Too heavy," he murmured, resting his forehead against her shoulder as he dragged in air.

"If you are, I'll say so."

"Just for a minute, then." He sank down hesitantly, still partly braced on his arms.

She tried to bring him closer. "You can do better than that."

"What about the baby?"

"The baby's fine."

"Okay, then." He relaxed fully, his solid weight pressing her into the mattress, his cheek against her shoulder.

He *was* heavy, but his deep sigh and whispered *thank you* was worth being slightly uncomfortable. She continued to caress his back.

Under her gentle ministrations, he sighed again and relaxed even more. Good. Except he was growing heavier. He was... *going to sleep*. And she couldn't breathe.

She jiggled his shoulder. "Seth."

No response except for a soft snore.

She jiggled harder. "*Seth.*"

Nothing.

If she didn't wake him soon, she would run out of air. She pinched his earlobe.

He jerked awake. "What the—" Pushing himself up on his outstretched arms, he blinked and glanced down at her, his expression sheepish. "I fell asleep, didn't I? I'm so sorry."

"I lured you into it. You tried to warn me you'd be too heavy, but I didn't believe you."

His expression changed to one of masculine pride. "Am I heavier than, um, what you've experienced before?"

"Yes."

"A lightweight, was he?" He smiled.

"Compared to you."

His smile widened. "Scrawny?"

"No." She started laughing. "He just doesn't spend his days riding, training horses and shoveling manure, so naturally he doesn't have your—"

"Powerful muscles?" He flexed his pecs.

"You're incorrigible."

"And heavy." He waggled his eyebrows at her. "Very heavy."

"So I discovered when I couldn't breathe."

Alarm flashed in his eyes. "Are you okay? Is the baby okay?"

"We're both fine. Trust me, I wouldn't have silently suffocated under your manly weight. If pinching your ear hadn't worked, I would have tried something more aggressive."

"Like what?"

"I'm pretty sure if I clamped my thighs together, I'd squeeze your—"

He winced. "Yes, ma'am, you would. My happy boys are nestled right between your lovely thighs. I thank you for choosing to pinch my ear before you went for the nutcracker move."

"I wouldn't have done it. I'm teasing you. I—" She smothered a yawn. "I would have pulled your hair next."

"I saw that yawn. Considering I just fell asleep on you, it's time to turn off the lights." He slipped free and climbed out of bed.

Propped on her elbow, she surveyed her naked cowboy from behind. He had the classic build of an athlete—broad shoulders tapering to narrow hips and muscular thighs. Nice. "When are you leaving town?"

"I'm due back the day after Christmas." He switched off the lamp on that side.

"Four more days, then."

"And four romantic nights." He turned and walked over to the nightstand on the far side of the bed. The glow highlighted his chiseled features as he leaned down and doused the light.

"I'm looking forward to each one."

"So am I." He rounded the bed and slid in beside her. "Especially since I won't be saying a permanent goodbye in four days. I tried to imagine that." He reached for her. "Thought I should prepare myself in case that turned out to be your decision."

She snuggled into his arms. "How'd that go?"

"Terrible." He brushed his lips over her forehead. "Especially when I thought about coming back to visit my aunt and cousins. Maybe I'll spend time with my half brothers if we get along. But if I wasn't allowed to spend time with you, that would be very sad."

"Just so you're prepared that I'll get bigger and bigger." And that she'd be leaving town in April.

He placed his hand over her baby bump. "That'll be exciting."

"It will? I mean, I'm excited, but that's different."

He spread his fingers and pressed gently. "I'm fascinated with the idea of a new human growing right there. Isn't it amazing?"

"Uh-huh." And he was starting to make her nervous. Making love was one thing. His active interest in her baby was setting off warning bells. If he got emotionally invested in her, things would go downhill fast. She placed her hand over his. "We should get some sleep."

"Yeah, I'd rather not think about why."

"Sorry." Or maybe she was overreacting. His interest might be a distraction from his own anxiety.

"It's okay. It's not like I've forgotten about it. Listen, are you comfortable like this? Or would you rather—"

"You know what I'd love?" The cozy setting called to her, pushing aside her worry.

"Name it."

"If I turn on my side with my back to you, then—"

"I'll spoon you. Perfect."

Once she was on her side, he curled his body protectively around hers and drew her closer. She fell asleep with his calloused hand cupping her belly.

* * *

An unfamiliar chime sounded in the darkness, waking her from a dream about a naked baby lying in a nest of twigs, waving its chubby arms. Not hard to identify where that came from.

Seth rolled over and tapped his phone, stopping the chime. Then he turned back and kissed her on the shoulder. "Rise and shine, pretty lady."

She shifted to face him. "How're you doing?"

"Okay. Wish I didn't feel so much like Gary Cooper in *High Noon*."

"Aw." She cradled his bristly face in both hands. "It'll work out just fine."

"Hope so. Ready for the light?"

"Go for it." She shielded her eyes when he reached for the lamp. Then she blinked as her pupils adjusted to the brightness. When she looked at Seth, he was smiling at her. "I have major bedhead, right?"

"You have major cuteness." He stood. "And sex appeal." He gestured to his stiff cock. "Better get out of here while you still can."

"Damn." She sucked in a breath as moisture rushed to her lady parts. "I didn't factor in this scenario."

"Too late, now." He stepped away from the bed. "Take off before my sense of responsibility evaporates in the heat of your sexiness."

She scrambled out of bed and made tracks for the connecting door. "I'll be in the shower if you need me for anything."

"Yeah, that was the wrong thing to say."

"I meant... oh, never mind!" She scurried into her room, but she left both doors open.

She hurried through her shower, quickly dried her hair and dressed. The aroma of coffee drifted from downstairs. Aunt Mo was up and starting breakfast. She needed to get down there. Crossing to the open doors between their two rooms, she rapped on the frame. "Can I come in?"

"Absolutely." He'd made his bed and he was dressed except for the long-sleeved denim shirt he held in his hand. "Glad for the company." He shoved his arms into the sleeves.

"You nicked yourself shaving."

"Yeah." He grimaced and plucked off the small piece of tissue on his chin. "Is it still bleeding?"

"No." She walked over and smoothed a hand over his freshly-shaven cheek. "You smell good."

"You, too." He cupped her face in both hands. "I want to kiss you, but I might never stop."

"And we both have things to do." She backed away from him. "Do you want coffee before you leave? And maybe a cinnamon roll? I could—"

"I'd better skip it. I'm jittery enough as it is."

"Will you text me when you get a chance?"

"Yes, ma'am." She rattled off her number and he entered it in his phone. "Can you please tell Aunt Mo that I went out to the ranch to help with the morning chores?" He unfastened his jeans, tucked in his shirt and zipped and buttoned his jeans again.

"I will."

"Appreciate it." He grabbed his coat and hat off the back of the chair in the corner and pocketed his keys and wallet. "That's it."

"I'll walk down with you."

"Thanks." He started toward the door, but turned back. "Guess I need one kiss, after all." He drew her into his arms. His kiss was gentle, almost reverent. Lifting his head, his gaze held hers. "Wish me luck."

Her heart ached for him. *Please let this be all he wants it to be.* "You know I do."

He took a deep breath. "Time to go."

15

Seth's truck felt a little empty without Zoe in it, but this was a solo job. He ought to feel right at home tackling this on his own. He'd been doing it all his life.

But Zoe's support and a taste of McGavin hospitality had pierced the self-sufficiency he'd cultivated over the years. He could resurrect it, though, with a little help from his friend Johnny. His truck was old enough to have a CD player in it and he kept some favorite albums in the console.

As he drove toward the two-lane in the pale light of dawn, he fished a Johnny Cash album from the console and slid it into the player. He had the album on his phone, but his truck had better speakers. Besides, listening to a CD was retro and after all, he was traveling back in time.

He sang along with *Ring of Fire* and *Don't Take Your Guns to Town*. He had his badass attitude going on until he turned off on the road to Wild Creek Ranch.

He gave up singing and shut off the CD player. Tough to sing when he had his throat in his mouth.

He clung to everything Zoe had said about this meeting with his dad. She had confidence that it would turn out well for everyone concerned, especially him. But she would say that, wouldn't she?

He reverted to deep-breathing techniques as he rounded the bend and the ranch house appeared, smoke drifting from the chimney. His truck was a mess from the trip down here. He should have figured out a plan to wash it. A little late to be worrying about that.

White-knuckling the steering wheel kept his hands from shaking as he down-shifted and aimed the truck toward the barn. He slowed to a crawl. As agitated as he was, he could make that classic brake/gas pedal mistake and smash into the antique structure.

The barn door was open and he quickly looked away. If by some weird coincidence his father had decided to help with feeding, he didn't want to know. At least not until he'd parked the truck, shut off the engine and stopped hyperventilating.

He pulled up to the barn, stepped carefully on the brake, turned off the ignition and dragged in several long, slow breaths. He could do this. Zoe believed in him. But mostly, he believed in himself. He'd managed without a father for thirty-one years. If this didn't work out, he'd be okay.

He'd left the diary in his room but the pictures lay on the passenger seat. He'd leave them there until after he'd talked with Kendra. As he opened the door and climbed down, the theme for *High Noon* played in his head. *Do Not Forsake Me.* Melodramatic, much? He sincerely needed to get over himself.

He sucked in another lungful of cold Montana air before leaving the protection of his truck and striking out for the open barn door. He buttoned his shearling jacket, turned up the collar and shoved his hands in his pockets.

The warmth of the barn, coupled with the familiar sights and smells of feeding time, calmed him. Cody was dishing out hay flakes from a wheelbarrow at the front of the aisle between the stalls and Aunt Kendra was doing the same at the far end with a second wheelbarrow. The horses stomped and snorted with impatience.

"Hey, Seth!" Cody gave him a smile.

"Greetings, Seth!" Aunt Kendra called out.

"Good morning, ma'am!"

Cody shoved back his hat. "Mom said you wanted to come and help, but aren't you supposed to be on vacation?"

"You know how it is. You get used to seeing horses every morning. Starts the day off right."

"Hate to admit it, but I'm the same." He gestured toward the wheelbarrow. "How about taking over here, and I'll head to the other barn?"

"That works. Just the hay flakes?"

"That's it." He took off a glove and held out his hand. "Appreciate the help, dude."

"You bet." Seth shook his hand, pulled gloves out of his pocket and set to work. When he and Aunt Kendra had closed the gap so she didn't have to shout, she invited him to stay for breakfast.

"Thank you, ma'am. That would be great."

"Aren't you missing Maureen's big Sunday breakfast? I think she even serves champagne."

"She might be. No matter. I've never been a fan of champagne first thing in the morning." He delivered hay to Jake and paused to give the big bay a friendly pat. "I sure did enjoy the ride yesterday."

"Thanks. It was a perfect day for it. Zoe took to it like a duck to water. I hope she comes back."

"She might." He'd ask her next time he made the trip.

Aunt Kendra delivered her last hay flake. "That takes care of this barn. We'll turn 'em out after breakfast, if you want to stick around."

"I'd enjoy that."

"Then let's stow the wheelbarrows and get on up to the house. I crave another cup of coffee."

His pulse rate picked up. He was minutes away, now. He followed her to the back of the barn, leaned his wheelbarrow against the wall next to hers, and sucked in a breath. "Before we leave the barn, there's something I need to mention."

She faced him. "I wondered if there might be."

His chest tightened. "You know how everyone keeps saying I look like Aleck?"

Her eyes widened. "Yeah."

"There's a reason for that."

Her hand went to her mouth. "*Hamish*?"

He nodded.

"Oh, my God. You're—"

"Helen's son. Yes."

"Did she ever—"

"No."

"Wow. Oh, Seth." She pressed a hand to her chest and took a deep breath. "Let me think." She bowed her head for a moment. "Okay, here's what we'll do. You stay here. I'll send him down."

"Okay." He sounded like he'd been running a race.

Her gaze warmed. "You're my nephew."

"Yes, ma'am."

She opened her arms. "Welcome to the family."

Family. He stood perfectly still as she wrapped her arms around him, then returned the hug as she gave him a tight squeeze. His throat closed.

She stepped away and swiped at her eyes. "I can't wait for my boys to hear about this. And Aleck and Rory. But I won't say a word until you've had a chance to... okay, I'm going now." She backed a few more steps down the aisle. "Stay right here. Don't go anywhere."

"I won't."

"Wow. What a Christmas." Then she turned and hurried out of the barn.

He closed his eyes and took several long, deep breaths. Oh, great. Now he was dizzy. And shaking. He walked down to Jake's stall. The gelding was intent on his hay, just like all the rest of them. They wouldn't appreciate him interrupting their breakfast just because he needed soothing.

Instead he paced the long length of the wooden aisle, his steps echoing in the cavernous space. He made three round-trips, not that he was counting or anything. He'd almost reached the back of the barn on his fourth one when a deep male voice called his name.

He turned. A man came toward him, his dark hair graying at the temples, his plaid jacket predominately green and dark blue.

He was about Seth's height and build. He held out his hand. "This day's been a long time comin', lad." His brogue was thick but understandable.

Seth grasped his father's hand and gazed into the same green eyes he saw every day when he shaved. His father's grip was firm, warm.

"How's your mother?" He pronounced it *mither.*

A chill traveled up his spine. "My mother?"

"Helen."

"She's... she died fourteen months ago."

His father gasped. "*Nay.*"

"It was unexpected. And quick."

His shoulders sagged. "That's ghastly news." He regarded Seth with compassion. "I'm so sorry, lad. Ye must be..." He waved his hand in the air. "What a tragedy."

"Yes and no." At least his father had remembered her. And was mourning her now. He got points for that. "If she hadn't died, I still wouldn't know about you."

He blinked. "What's that you say?"

"She told me nothing. My father could have been the mailman for all I knew."

"She *never* told you? Why the devil not?"

"She said it was too painful to discuss."

His father stared at him in confusion. "I dunna understand."

He could explain, or he could protect his mother's feelings. "I think she was afraid I'd save my money and run off to Scotland looking for you." Partly true. "I was all she had." Very true. "She decided keeping the details to herself was best for all concerned."

"How'd you find out, then?"

"Her diary."

He nodded and his gaze dropped to the scarred wood beneath his feet. "I remember she kept one." He was silent for a while, and when he glanced up, his eyes were moist.

Seth's throat tightened and he glanced away.

"She never married, then?"

"She had me. She used to say having no stepfather is better than putting up with a loser." *And she could never love another man the way she'd loved you.*

He swallowed. "I can see her figuring that out. She was loyal to the core." He looked at Seth and shook his head. "You dunna ken how many times for the next couple of years after I left Helen I second-guessed m'self about whether I should've stayed in Eagles Nest. She would never have come to Scotland."

His heart ached for his mother. If his father had made contact, would things have turned out different? "But then you met someone."

"Aye. Greer is my soulmate, no question about it." His chest heaved. "But I would give anythin' if Helen had told me about you. All those years, wasted. You could have come over, made friends with your half-brothers..." He trailed off, focused on the row of stalls. "Such a waste."

But sharing her son with the man she'd loved and his new wife would have been very tough. Any remaining resentment toward her melted. She'd given her heart away even though a happy-ever-after was impossible. How could he judge her decision to wall off the pain?

His father swung to face him, his expression resolute. "What's done is done, right? We'll pick up the threads and move on. Aleck and Rory live here, so that's easy."

He tensed. "But they might not care to—"

"Ach, lad." He waved a hand. "Don't bother yourself about that. My boys will be mostly curious. They'll just want t'get a look at ye."

"What about your wife?"

"Greer knows. The name Turner was my clue. I told her who ye were before I came down here."

"What did she say?"

"She's the salt of the Earth. She's aware I was no choir boy before we met. She takes me as I am."

The pressure in his chest eased. "Then you're a lucky man."

"Aye, that I am, lad. If you ever find a lass who loves you, warts and all, hang on tight."

"I'll remember that."

His father grinned. "That's what a da's supposed t'do, y'know. Impart all our great wisdom to our bairn."

"Is that so?" His father's smile... so like his own. The years had permanently etched the crinkles at the corners of his eyes and the creases on his cheeks. This face would be his in twenty years.

"Here's another piece of wisdom. Take everythin' I say with a grain of salt. I dunna ken nearly what I think I do."

"Me, either." He held his father's gaze. So familiar.

"Seein' yourself, lad?"

He nodded. "It's trippy."

"Aye. I'm seein' m'self from years back. I'm surprised Kendra dinna ken who ye were much earlier. Spittin' image. More than Aleck. Dunna see much of your ma in you, though."

"I have... I brought some snapshots."

"Of m'self and your ma?"

"Yes. They're—"

"I'd love t'see 'em."

"I left them in the truck. Be right back."

"I'll walk with ye."

"Okay." His dad's stride matched his. Freaky.

"Ye work as a cowboy, then?"

"I do."

"Thought so." As they stepped outside, he gestured to the truck. "Rory's got one like this."

"Probably a lot cleaner than mine."

"Nay. Dirtier. Who cares if it ferries you around gud and proper?"

"True." He opened the passenger door and the pictures fluttered in a sudden gust of wind. One drifted to the floorboard. He picked it up and gathered the rest as another icy blast whipped around the truck.

"I'm chitterin'. Let's get in."

"Sure, okay." He left the door open and carried the pictures around to the driver's side. The cab had cooled off fast. He started the engine and the heater came on.

"Ah, much better." His father rubbed his hands together. "Should've worn the hat Kendra offered, but I looked like a numptie."

"You were worried about what I'd think?"

"'Course I was. Dinna want your first impression of your ol' da to be a bad one. Though ye might think I'm an eejit for not wearin' a hat."

"I didn't think that. I was too busy worrying about the impression I'd make on you."

He chuckled. "What a pair of bampots."

"What's that? I can guess, but—"

"An eejit." He glanced across the console. "Guess we must be related."

Seth laughed. "Guess so."

* * *

The pictures inspired Seth's father to reminisce about his life as a young man in Eagles Nest, an inexperienced guy dazzled by Helen

Turner, who was slightly older and living on her own in nearby Bozeman.

A chime from his phone lying on the console interrupted a daring tale about tubing the rapids in Wild Creek.

His father glanced over at the house. "More trucks up there, now. How long have we been talkin'?"

Seth picked up his phone. "About an hour. Kendra's asking how soon we'll be done."

"An hour already? Canna be." He dug his phone out and tapped it. "Greer's askin' the same thing. Dinna hear her text."

Seth sent a quick answer to Kendra and tucked the phone in his jacket pocket. "I told her we're on our way. Buckle up. I'll drive us to the house."

"Brilliant." His father fastened his seatbelt as Seth put the truck in reverse. "Powerful engine."

"I wanted something that could haul a horse trailer."

"Ye have a horse, then?"

"Not yet. But I will." He'd let that dream slide, too. Time for a place of his own, a horse of his own, and… a family of his own? Maybe so.

He swung the truck around and drove toward the house. "Who takes the ball when we walk in?"

"I'd be honored to introduce ye as my son, but since ye had the baws to search out your kinfolk, I'll yield to—"

"I'd like you to introduce me as your son."

"Aye, that's more elegant." His voice was suspiciously husky. "Ye will be needin' information on Clan McGavin soon. This jacket is McGavin plaid."

"The McGavins have a tartan?"

"Aye."

"Kilts?"

"Aye."

"I'll be damned." He parked the truck.

"What about these?" His father held up the pictures. "Take 'em in?"

"Will they upset anybody?"

"Nay. They're part of our family history. I'd like to make copies." He tucked the pictures carefully in his jacket pocket and climbed out of the truck.

Adrenalin pumping, Seth walked to the house beside his father. *Part of our family history.* A simple statement loaded with implications. Until now, his family history had consisted of his mom and him.

As he mounted the steps, his boots hitting the planks in unison with the man next to him, someone inside yelled *they're here* and the massive front door opened.

He stood back. His father squared his shoulders and lifted his chin before striding into the house. Seth followed and closed the door behind him.

When he turned around, his eyes widened. So many folks. Some he'd met but most he hadn't. His half-brothers were easy to spot, a redhead and a guy who looked eerily like him.

Had to be at least twenty people in the room. All family. *His* family.

His father cleared his throat and spoke with calm authority. "As your clan chief, I'm honored to present our newest member of Clan McGavin, my son, Seth Turner."

He glanced at his half-brothers. They each gave him a quick grin and a nod. A fiftyish redhead standing near them had to be Greer. She sent him a warm smile. His gaze swept the room and they were *all* smiling. Every single person.

His father touched his arm. "Seth, would you like to say a few words to your family?"

Oh, God. He misted up and his throat tightened. He managed a hoarse, "I'm honored to be here."

"Let's hear it for Seth!" The voice had a military ring to it. Ryker. The room erupted in cheers.

Seth's vision blurred. Ducking his head, he blinked several times. *Steady, Turner.* He sniffed and glanced up just as everyone headed toward him with Kendra in the lead.

She enveloped him in a hug. "Welcome home."

Heck, now he was blinking and sniffing again. Oh, well. Guess it was okay for everyone to see him tearing up. They were family.

16

Aunt Mo's only reference to Zoe's night with Seth was a brief comment that she looked happy. Neither of them had time to chat, anyway. Aunt Mo had her hands full cleaning up after the elaborate Sunday breakfast and Zoe had tackled the housecleaning chores on her own today.

By pushing herself, she managed to finish before noon. She was in the middle of a yoga pose when Seth's text arrived. Stepping off her mat, she picked up her phone.

Everything's great here. Staying for lunch. I'll be back in plenty of time to go to the talent show with you and your aunt. By the way, you're welcome to tell her why I went to the ranch this morning if you want to.

She sent a quick reply letting him know how happy she was for him. Leaving her room, she hurried downstairs and found Aunt Mo at her desk making a shopping list. "Looks like you're heading into town."

"I am. Want to go along? We could grab lunch at Pie in the Sky."

"I'd love that. Would you have time to stop at the Western wear store?"

Her aunt smiled. "A gift for a certain cowboy?"

"Yes. It's perfect timing since he's not here."

"He's still out at the ranch?"

"He is. I'll tell you about it on the way. I just need to change out of my yoga pants." Ten minutes later, she was in the passenger seat of Aunt Mo's SUV. "What do you need to buy?"

"I could use some more serving platters, and this close to Christmas, something like that will be on sale. Pills and Pop might have their gift bags and boxes on sale, too. I like to put a little something in everyone's room on Christmas Eve and I'm low on small containers."

"What a nice idea. I give all the yoga students a discount coupon for January classes, but I just put it in an envelope. Maybe next year I'll dress it up."

"Those little touches mean a lot when you're running a small business. Or any business, for that matter. But never mind that. What's up with Seth?"

"Now I'm wondering if I should blurt it out while you're driving."

"I think you'd better, or I'll die of curiosity and you'll have to take the wheel."

"Okay. He came to Eagles Nest for Christmas because he read his late mother's diary and discovered he's a McGavin."

"Oh, my God! Tell me all!"

Zoe filled in the details.

"Everything's straightened out, now? He's a part of the family?"

"That's what it sounds like."

"That's good. He's a sweetie. He'll fit right in with the rest of the McGavins. When did you find this out?"

"Friday night on the way to the GG."

"Whew. This is… epic. I've been looking forward to the talent show, but now I'm *really* looking forward to the talent show. All the players will be there and now the secret's out. Nothing beats small-town drama."

"I wouldn't know. I haven't been here long enough. But that reminds me—you don't have to keep my pregnancy a secret anymore, now that it's becoming more obvious. I plan to tell people that I'm looking forward to raising the baby on my own."

"Short and to the point."

"Exactly what I'm going for."

"I just thought of something. If Seth's related to Kendra and her boys, he'll want to come back and visit."

"I'm sure he will."

"And visit you, too?"

"He wants to, and it would seem weird if he drove down and I didn't see him."

"Hm."

"I've made it crystal clear I'm going back to Milwaukee after the baby's born, and he understands. But it would be pointless not to enjoy each other's company until then."

"I'm glad you've talked it through." She snagged a parking spot in front of Pie in the Sky. "Let's get some lunch and a box of Christmas goodies for our ravenous guests."

Three hours later, they came home with Aunt Mo's platters, plenty of gift bags and boxes, a rawhide-patterned, fringed Onesie for a newborn that would work for a boy or a girl, and a plaid Western shirt for Seth in Christmas colors. She'd guessed at the size, but after spending a night in bed with him, her guess was likely accurate.

Seth's truck was in the parking lot when they returned. Her pulse rate jacked up.

She asked Aunt Mo to add Seth's shirt in with her packages before they walked into the reception area. He wasn't there, so she gave her aunt a hug, left her parka on the hook by the door and hurried upstairs.

Seth stepped out into the hall when she was halfway there. He'd taken off his denim shirt and his boots, leaving on his jeans, socks and a white T-shirt. "It is you! I thought I recognized your footsteps."

Her heart squeezed at the joy in his expression. "Went shopping with Aunt Mo."

"What'd you get?" He walked to meet her.

"Just a little something for the baby." She was out of breath and so glad to see him it wasn't funny.

"Let's see it."

"Found it at the Western Wear store." She pulled the fringed outfit out of the bag.

He grinned. "That's way too cute." He held it up. "Will the baby really be that small?"

"Newborns are tiny."

"I wouldn't know. I don't think I've ever been around one. Whole bunch of bachelors at the ranch where I work. But this outfit is hysterical.

What's it called?" He peered at the label. "A Onesie? What's that mean?"

"I guess it refers to it being all one piece instead of two. I picked this one because it works for a boy or a girl."

"Good thinking." He handed it back to her. "You planning to raise a little cowboy or cowgirl?"

"We'll see. This outfit seemed like a fun idea for a baby born in Montana, though. Enough about baby clothes." She tucked her purchase back in the bag. "I want to hear all about Wild Creek!"

"Then step into my parlor." He gestured toward his open door. "Make yourself comfortable."

She smiled as she walked past him into the room. "But not too comfortable. We'll need to leave for the GG in about forty-five minutes." Judging from the depressed spot on the comforter and the pillows stacked against the headboard, he'd been propped up against them reading his book. His phone lay on the bed, too.

"You can at least take off your boots and join me on the bed." He gave her an innocent look. "For ease of conversation."

She laughed. "I could do that." She toed off her boots and walked around the bed, climbing in on the side that had no body imprint. They could just relax and talk, right? Just because this bed had been the location of previous orgasmic bliss didn't mean it couldn't be treated like a living room sofa.

"I'll just close the door so our conversation won't be interrupted."

The click of the latch sent moisture rushing to significant parts of her increasingly hot body. "I really do want to hear about your time at Wild Creek." Grabbing one of his pillows, she used it as a cushion, leaned back and crossed her arms. There.

"And I really do want to tell you." He moved his phone to the bedside table. "Right after I kiss you hello." He crawled onto the bed and over toward her, putting a knee on either side of her hips before he sat back on his heels and smiled. "I haven't seen you for a long time."

"I don't think this is a very good idea."

"I think it's a wonderful idea." He grasped her by the shoulders. "I just need you to uncross your arms and lean toward me."

"You know what's going to happen if we start kissing."

"We'll both be very happy."

"One kiss." She uncrossed her arms and slid her palms up the soft cotton of his T-shirt.

He sucked in a breath and his muscles contracted beneath her touch. Slowly he leaned in, as he gently massaged her shoulders. "I've been craving this all day."

"Me, too."

"I wanted to stay for lunch at the ranch, but I also wanted to be with you." Sliding his hands along her shoulders, he cupped her face in both hands. "It was a tough call."

"You made the right one."

He brushed his thumbs over her cheekbones. "I'm invited for Christmas dinner."

"That's lovely. Just what you wanted. A table full of people you care about."

"That's why I asked to bring you and your aunt."

"Oh, but we're not—"

"They're thrilled with the idea. And I want you there, Zoe. Please say you'll come with me."

Christmas dinner with his family? Wouldn't that brand them as a couple?

"You'll come, right?"

"Let me ask Aunt Mo." A cowardly dodge, but the best she could do.

"We'll ask her tonight." His gaze drifted to her mouth. "And now for my kiss." Closing the distance between them, he settled his lips over hers.

As always, his mouth commanded her full attention, coaxing her to enjoy every lusty temptation he offered. But now he'd added something more—a boldness, a strengthened confidence that was wildly arousing. Any hesitation or uncertainty was gone.

He was claiming his power. The visit to Wild Creek had been good for him. And oh, he would be so good for her right now. Her body was ready to give him everything and anything he wanted.

He drew back, breathing hard. "I want you so much."

She opened her eyes and trembled at the fire in his. "We'll be fast."

"No. I don't want fast." His chest heaved. "I don't want to rush through making love to you and then rush to get ready in time. We'll be back in this bed tonight. I can wait."

She took a shaky breath, tried to get her bearings. Saying no to a quickie seemed like another warning sign. But she couldn't very well argue that point right now. "So tell me about Wild Creek."

"I'd better move to my side of the bed or I won't be able to remember any of it." He repositioned himself. "I have more pillows than you." He gave her one.

"Thanks."

"First off, my father, or my da, as they say in Scotland, is clan chief of the McGavins." He picked up his phone and scrolled through his pictures. "Here he is."

"Wow. He does look like an older version of you. Very distinguished. I can see him as clan chief."

"He says they're still working on making it official, but he's in line, so he's claiming it. I'm the son of a clan chief. How cool is that?"

"Very cool. Can I look through these?"

"By all means."

"Is this your stepmother?" She held up the phone. "The red-haired lady?"

"Yes, that's Greer. She asked me to call her *ma,* which works for me because that's different from *mom*, so I don't have to make any mental shifts."

She continued to scroll through the pictures. "And here you are with your half-brothers. I just realized—you're the eldest son! Does that put you in line to be clan chief?"

"I think so, but that's years down the road. My da's in good health. Aleck didn't seem upset about losing that spot, but we'll talk. If he wants it, I can abdicate, or whatever it is you do."

"It's a whole other world over there, isn't it?"

"Seems like it. I want to visit. What a kick listening to the way they talk. Everything they like is *pure barry*, and everything they don't like is *rank.*"

"I've heard Aleck and Rory come out with both of those. And when they're having a discussion they're having *a right ol' blether.*"

"Yep, that's how my da described our conversation down at the barn. Or rather, our conversation in my truck. We had to get out of the cold. His wool jacket is McGavin plaid, which is why he wore it to meet me, but he needs a shearling one for Montana."

She handed back his phone. "The pictures are great. This couldn't have turned out any better if you'd planned it all on purpose."

"They were all saying it was meant to be." He reached for her hand and laced his fingers through hers. "Like us. I think we were destined to meet."

More alarm bells. "Seth, I'm going back to Milwaukee in April."

"I know. But we're intelligent people. We'll figure it out."

No, they wouldn't. There was nothing to figure out. He would stay in Montana where he had family. She would return to Milwaukee, to *her* family and the business she loved that would support her baby's future.

He was on a high from a wonderful day with his newly discovered relatives. He wasn't thinking straight. She'd remind him of that later.

<u>17</u>

Seth hadn't grasped the whole picture when he'd offered to escort Zoe and Aunt Mo to the talent show. His truck only carried one passenger. Consequently, Aunt Mo drove her SUV with Zoe in the front and him in the back.

But when it turned out they'd have to park down the street and walk almost two blocks to the GG, he asserted himself. It took some discussion to get Aunt Mo to relent and drive up to the front door so she and Zoe could go straight in. She handed over her keys and gave him a kiss on the cheek.

He was getting a lot of those today. Nice. He parked her car in a space they'd spotted earlier, and set out on foot.

He'd hang onto the keys so he could fetch the car when the event was over. Turning his collar up, he dipped his head and anchored his hat with one hand. That was some wind. His da might label it *jeelit* or *pure Baltic* but he was so excited about the evening ahead that nothing fazed him.

During lunch the group had given him a few hints about the acts he'd see and he couldn't wait. Aunt Kendra had clued him in about the

Whine and Cheese Club, her gal pals who would be performing together. The McGavins would have a special seating section next to the tables occupied by Quinn's kinfolk, the Sawyers. As if one family wasn't enough, he'd become an honorary member of the Sawyers, too.

The legendary Badger Calhoun would be there, along with the Bennetts, also part of the inner circle. While he'd waited for Zoe to come home he'd made copious notes on his phone, which he'd tucked in an inside pocket of his coat. Thank goodness he'd remembered to charge it because he'd be taking more pictures tonight.

He joined the growing crowd of folks who hadn't found a space in the parking lot, either.

Someone called his name and he turned. Trevor, the only cousin he hadn't met until this morning, came hurrying toward him, hand-in-hand with Olivia, his fiancée.

He clapped Seth on the shoulder. "What are you doing wandering out here all alone, cuz?"

"Hey, Trevor. Nice to see you again, Olivia." He tipped his hat but kept a grip on it. He'd seen a couple of other Stetsons rolling down the sidewalk. "I let Zoe and Aunt Mo off at the door. Parked down the street."

"Us, too, but Olivia refused to let me drop her off." He grinned at his bride-to-be as they all hurried through the parking lot to the front door. "Stubborn woman."

"Women tolerate cold better than men," Olivia said. "It's a scientific fact. You should let me drop *you* off."

Trevor laughed. "My mom would have something to say about that."

"I know she would," Olivia said, "so this is my compromise move. Speaking of Kendra, she couldn't stop raving about you after you left, Seth."

That counteracted the cold air just fine. "That's great to hear. What an experience, walking into that living room and seeing you all there."

"It was a small miracle that everybody made it," Trevor said. "I was on call at the fire department. Ryker had to switch flight assignments with Badger. Mandy finished her work on tonight's costumes about thirty minutes before she got the call from my mom."

"And then my da and I kept you all waiting."

"That just built the suspense," Olivia said. "And the climactic moment was perfect. I had no idea Hamish was a clan chief. Gave me chills when he announced that."

Trevor nodded. "Lots of talk about setting up a group trip to go over there. *Montana McGavins Invade Scotland.* Something like that. You in?"

"You know it. Hey, look at that, we're here."

"Brace yourself, cuz. You've never seen anything like this."

"Ah, no need to brace myself. I'm diving in headfirst." He held the door for Trevor and Olivia and followed them inside the GG.

What a difference from the first time he'd walked in, riddled with anxiety at the prospect of meeting his half-brothers. Taking his phone from his pocket, he gave his hat and jacket to the coat check attendant. Either that was a new wrinkle for this event or he'd missed it last time. He scanned the crowd. Aleck and Rory, dressed in their plaids, rose to their feet and waved him over.

Zoe and Aunt Mo, tucked in with the McGavin contingent, had drinks in front of them. Tables had been pushed together and nearly everyone who'd been at the ranch today was already here. His ma and da sat beaming at him as he wound his way through the crowd. If this was some crazy dream, he never wanted to wake up.

An empty chair between Zoe and Aunt Mo likely belonged to him, but he chose to go around greeting everybody before claiming it. If that made him a dork, so be it. He was too happy to care.

He shook hands and gave hugs to all the McGavins first, and after that Quinn introduced him to his three sons, his daughter, and everyone's partner. Aunt Kendra stepped in next and led him to the Bennett table, where he finally met Badger.

Placing his napkin on the table, Badger rose, turned and looked Seth up and down. "Bless my soul, if it isn't the fabled Seth Turner." He held out his hand and clapped him on the shoulder. "We meet at last."

"You've heard of me?" He shook Badger's hand.

"Are you kiddin'? The way y'all have been galivantin' around town like an animated version of *Where's Waldo,* I'd be hard-pressed to find anybody who *hasn't* heard of y'all."

"Zoe and I had some vital reconnaissance work to do."

Badger nodded. "Copy that."

"I've heard a lot about you, too."

"Believe the good parts, ignore the bad." He shoved his hands in his pockets and rocked back on his boot heels. "Just out of curiosity, though, what've y'all heard?"

Seth laughed. He'd make sure he saw more of this guy. "That you're a force of nature."

"Well, that's gratifyin'. At least that message is gettin' through. Listen, if you ever—"

Aunt Kendra tugged on Seth's sleeve. "We need to get back to the table. Food's coming."

"Uh-oh. I haven't ordered."

"It's an abbreviated menu. We ordered for you."

"Okay, then." He held out his hand for another shake because Badger was a two-handshake kind of guy. "Gotta go, but we'll have to do this again sometime."

"I'll look forward to it. If you ever need any help with recon, look me up. I'm an expert."

"Will do." He was still chuckling when he squeezed into his seat between Zoe and Aunt Mo. "Tight quarters."

"Yep." Zoe glanced at him. "You just met Badger."

"How'd you know?"

"You're laughing. He has that effect on everybody. Did you have fun making the rounds?"

"More than you can imagine."

"You looked like a celebrity schmoozing with his fans."

He groaned. "I didn't mean to turn it into—"

"No, no, that was meant as a compliment. You are somewhat of a celebrity in this small community."

"Why?"

Aunt Mo turned to him and joined the conversation. "In case you haven't noticed, it's a dramatic story—a handsome cowboy, the love child of Hamish McGavin, noble Highland clan chief, shows up to claim his place as the eldest son."

"I'm not claiming anything. Aleck can have it."

Aunt Mo smiled. "That kind of humble self-sacrifice will only add to your appeal."

He rolled his eyes.

"Go ahead and scoff if you want, but it's exciting."

"It is?"

"Oh, you know it, son. You're heir to the throne of a Highland clan chief. I'm picturing you standing resolute and proud on the Scottish moor, your McGavin plaid rippling in the wind."

He gazed at her in amusement. "Do tell?"

"Clearly you've never read a romance novel about men in kilts."

"That would be a no."

"Take my word for it. Women are suckers for a man in a kilt, especially if that man has a legitimate reason to wear the plaid."

"I'll keep that in mind." He glanced at Zoe. "Are you excited by all that?"

"Let's just say I'm not immune."

"Good to know." Although he didn't have anything in McGavin plaid yet, he was hooked into the source. If it would help his cause with Zoe, he would gladly wrap himself in as many yards of the stuff as she required.

"I think that McGavin's Pale Ale is yours, by the way." Zoe gestured to the mug on the table that sat slightly to his right, almost in front of Aunt Mo. "People were ordering things right and left, so I'm not sure."

He glanced over at Zoe's aunt. "I'm told that mug might be mine, but I want to make sure you didn't order it for yourself."

"Thank you, but that's yours." Aunt Mo raised her glass of red wine. "This is my drink of choice. Did you find a place for my car?"

"It's safe and sound. I'll fetch it when the night's over."

"You're a good boy." She raised her glass in his direction.

He tapped his mug against it. "Thank you."

"Like I said yesterday, you remind me of my Bobby. You're not like him in looks. He was much older than you and about ten years older than me. But you're like him in spirit."

"I'm honored that you'd say that."

"Normally I wouldn't get into something so personal when I'm in a crowd, except this is my second glass of wine."

"I see."

"When you talked me into letting you park the SUV, I realized you would likely be driving us home, so if I want a little extra sip of wine, no problem."

"Drink up, Aunt Mo."

She gave him a sly look. "That's the first time you've called me that to my face."

"I had to ease into it."

"Brings us closer together, don't you think?"

"I do."

She leaned toward him. "Just so you know, when you come to visit Zoe, whenever that is..."

"I'll be back as often as I can manage it."

"Excellent. My plan is to switch her from her current room to yours. Which means when you come down for a visit, you can stay with her, free of charge."

"That's very generous, but I feel that I should pay."

"Here's the way I figure it. Kendra would let you stay at the ranch for nothing, and although that puts you in the heart of McGavin country, you'll be across town from Zoe."

"That's a good point. I'll gratefully accept your hospitality, then." If Aunt Mo wanted to play matchmaker, he'd be a fool to object.

18

Dinner was a rambunctious affair, with jokes flying, and in one instance, dinner rolls. Zoe had never laughed so hard during a meal, and Seth held his own, giving as good as he got from his cousins and half brothers.

For dessert, servers brought each table a large chocolate yule log to share, family style. Zoe watched in admiration as Kendra took charge of cutting the cake and swiftly dealt with any complaints about who got the larger piece or who had more frosting. At some point, she'd need to ask Kendra for child-rearing tips.

As the family finished their dessert, Bryce and Nicole walked up on stage playing and singing *Here Comes Santa Claus.* Dressed for glamour and impact, they wore bright red—boots, jeans, shirts and hats. Silver sequins glittered on the back pockets of their jeans, the yoke of their shirts and the band around their hats.

The audience greeted them with cheers and whistles. They finished up with a flourish, joined hands and bowed in graceful unison.

Then Nicole stepped up to the mic. "Merry Christmas, Eagles Nesters!"

Shouts of *Merry Christmas, Nicole* echoed in the large room.

She flipped back her curly red hair with one hand. "Who said redheads can't wear red?" She twirled to show off her outfit. "Once again, thank you Mandy McGavin, for all the gorgeous outfits you create for us." She swept a hand toward Mandy, who blushed as everyone applauded.

"Mandy also directed the making of all the fabulous costumes in the show, except for Warren Bennett's Godman spandex... uh... concoction. He gets all the credit for that."

Cries of *Go, Godman* and *Godman rules* erupted. One of them had a distinctive Southern drawl.

"I know you're all eager to find out what our talented folks have in store for you. Bryce and I will kick off the festivities with the fan favorite *All I Want for Christmas is You.* Let's get this party started!"

As they swung into the intro, Seth leaned over and murmured *great song* in her ear.

She nodded, and didn't object when he reached for her hand under the table. She and her folks watched *Love, Actually* every year at Christmas and the song was a prominent part of the movie. Hearing it made her wistful. Holding hands with Seth helped.

At the end of the number, the crowd showered Bryce and Nicole with wild applause. Coming down from the stage, they moved through the tables greeting everyone while Badger, Ryker and Cody set up their juggling act.

Mannheim Steamroller's *Deck the Halls* blasted from the GG's enhanced sound system and the broad-shouldered cowboys swung into action. Zoe held her breath as china Christmas plates sailed through the air.

With Badger anchoring the middle of the trio, they kept a dozen plates spinning—behind their backs, over their shoulders, and high in the air. When the music ended and they each held up four unbroken plates in triumph, the room exploded in stomping, cheering and whistling praise.

Seth squeezed Zoe's hand. "I want to learn that."

"It'll take plenty of practice."

He smiled. "Guess I might have to drive down here more often, then."

She had no time to respond to that because the six members of the Sawyer family had taken the stage. Quinn and his brother Brendan stood on either side of the four kids—Roxanne, Wes, Gage and Pete. Quinn blew one note on the pitch pipe and they launched into a rousing acapella rendition of *Carol of the Bells.*

When they finished, Zoe clapped until her hands hurt. "I'm *loving* this."

"Yeah, me, too." Seth looked awed. "I had no idea. I was thinking amateur talent show, but this…"

"Told you." Aunt Mo beamed at them. "Zoe, we're getting your mom and dad out here next year and to hell with my bottom line." Then she clapped her hand over her mouth and giggled. "Pardon my French."

Zoe reached over and squeezed her aunt's hand. "We'll plan on it." Which meant she'd be spending next Christmas in Eagles Nest. Guaranteed Seth would be here, too.

And so would her eight month old baby. Sobering thought.

Aunt Mo chuckled. "Here comes Ellie Mae Stockton for her number. She's always good for a laugh. I'll bet you haven't met her yet, Seth."

"No, ma'am."

"She's a clerk at Pills and Pop, our drugstore, and she's eighty-five if she's a day."

"I wouldn't mind having that outfit." Zoe loved dresses with skirts she could twirl in. The pattern on this one was multi-colored Christmas ornaments. "It would be great for dancing."

"I expect that's what she'll do," Aunt Mo said.

Little Saint Nick by the Beach Boys poured from the sound system and Ellie Mae began to dance while surveying the audience as if looking for someone. Leaving the stage, she sashayed between tables until she stood swaying in front of Seth.

He gazed up at her, evidently bemused.

Ellie Mae crooked her finger.

His eyebrows rose.

Grabbing his hand, she tugged. "Dance with me, cowboy," she crooned in time with the song.

He looked at Zoe, shrugged, and followed Ellie Mae up to the stage. Then he proceeded to execute a credible jitterbug, laughing and flirting with Ellie Mae the whole time. The crowd got into it, clapping in time with the beat and joining in with the chorus.

Adorable. Zoe's chest swelled with an emotion that had nothing to do with lust.

Aunt Mo leaned across the seat Seth had vacated. "He's a keeper, Zoe."

Yes. But not for me.

When the song ended, he bowed elaborately toward Ellie Mae. When he straightened, she grabbed his face and planted a kiss on his mouth. Then she scurried off the stage as the audience roared in approval.

Seth returned with lipstick on his mouth and was mobbed by the McGavin contingent. One of his cousins handed him a bandana and he used it to wipe away the lipstick before he took his seat.

Zoe gazed at him. "You were a hit."

"It was fun." He grinned. "She's a good dancer."

Aunt Mo gave him a nudge. "How about that? In town for three days and you're already in the Christmas talent show."

He laughed. "Maybe next year I'll be in it on purpose." He took a sip of his beer and recaptured Zoe's hand. "Can't think of a better place to be for the holidays." He glanced at her. "Right?"

"Right." Now was not the time for brutal honesty. In fact, it was a bad time to evaluate... anything.

The volunteer firefighters were up next to sing *Joy to the World*, with Trevor clearly in his element. After hearing him sing at the B&B, Zoe wasn't surprised.

After the firefighters received a rousing ovation, they turned the stage over to a middle-aged, balding man wearing a Superman-like suit, cape and all, except instead of a large *S* on his chest, the letter was *G*.

Aunt Mo clapped her hands together in delight. "It's Godman!"

"That's Reverend Bennett?" Zoe stared at the guy strutting around the stage, chest thrust out, hands on his hips as the audience chanted *Godman, Godman, Godman.*

"That's him." Her aunt practically bounced with excitement. "He's not like any minister you've ever seen before."

Which proved to be true. His standup routine was perfectly timed and contained some of the funniest jokes about religion she'd ever heard. She laughed until the tears came. "Does he talk like this in church?" she whispered to her aunt.

"Sometimes. He's a little more serious, there."

The end of Godman's performance was greeted with shouts, chanting and wild applause. He waved and left the stage.

"He's a riot." Seth cleared the hoarseness from his throat. "Never heard a preacher talk like that. Made me choke on my beer. I hope my da and my brothers could hear it even if they couldn't see it."

Zoe glanced to where they'd been sitting. "Where are they?" She'd caught that Seth had eliminated the *half* when referring to Aleck and

Rory. He was embracing his new family with his whole heart.

"They slipped out right as he got started. I'm guessing they're fetching their bagpipes and Rory's snare drum, maybe tuning up or whatever you do before you play one of those things."

"Oh."

"Badger went with them, so I guess he's playing the pipes, too. They must have tucked their instruments in a storeroom since they couldn't very well have them out here the whole time."

"So there will be three bagpipes and a snare drum?" Zoe frowned. "Won't that be kind of loud?"

"I think you'll be pleasantly surprised," Aunt Mo said. "Aleck knows how to tone it down and he's the one who taught Badger. I'll bet Hamish plays the same way."

Seth glanced toward the back of the room. "Here they come."

A muted rat-a-tat-tat of a snare drum announced the arrival of the four men, three wearing McGavin plaid and one in a tartan of a different color.

"I heard that Badger ordered the Calhoun plaid," Aunt Mo said.

"He must have changed into it just now, then," Seth said. "He didn't have it on before."

"This is his first time performing with it," Aunt Mo said. "Knowing Badger, he wanted to reveal the outfit at the last minute for greater impact."

Seth laughed. "Nothing wrong with a little flair."

"Oh, he has that. He's totally getting into his Scottish heritage."

"I plan on getting into mine." Seth winked at Zoe.

Once they were all on stage, Hamish stepped up to the mic. "It's a great honor to play for ye. I want to thank ye for the kindness shown to my lads, Aleck and Rory, these past few months. And for your warm welcome of my eldest, Seth. Tonight we'll be playin' *When a Child Is Born*."

"Oh, I love that song," Aunt Mo said. "Never heard it on bagpipes before."

Seth looked over at Zoe. "Know this one?"

She nodded. "It's lovely." And had more meaning for her tonight than ever before. From the first haunting notes, she was swept away, filling in lyrics that described a baby's birth as a message of hope.

Bagpipes weren't too loud for this song if the pipers knew what they were doing. These did. A hush fell over the crowd as the ancient instrument wove a spell of love and peace.

Closing her eyes, she let the melody wash over her and her unborn child. When she opened them again, Seth's warm gaze was on her, not his da and brothers. She had a problem.

Then the song ended and his attention shifted as he jumped to his feet to applaud his new-found family. The rest of the audience joined him, giving the pipers a standing ovation for creating a magical moment.

As it died down, Bryce returned to the mic. "It's become a tradition for the Whine and Cheese Club to perform the final number in our talent show. Usually the room's a madhouse after that, so I'll take this moment to thank each one of you for supporting our event. We raised a sizable amount of money and many Eagles Nest families who would have had a meager Christmas this year will have a bountiful one, instead. Give yourselves a hand."

Amid the resulting thunderous applause, Seth turned to Aunt Mo. "I didn't donate anything and I want to. Can I still do it?"

"I'm sure if you catch Bryce either tonight or in the next couple of days, he'll be happy to take whatever you care to give."

"I'll do that."

Bryce tapped the mic. "The ladies are getting impatient. I've been asked to explain that because they're performing Rudolph tonight, and Santa has eight reindeer plus Rudolph, they were short three participants. They want to thank Mandy, Faith and April for stepping into the breach. Oh, and Santa will be played by... well, I think you'll figure it out. Enjoy."

Gene Autry's familiar rendition began, with women in reindeer costumes prancing out with identifying signs around their necks. They wore full-body reindeer suits with a hood and antlers, but their faces were visible.

Aunt Mo looked over at Zoe. "I don't see Kendra, yet."

"Then she must be Rudolph."

Sure enough, Kendra showed up wearing a blinking red nose. On cue, the other reindeer shunned her. Then the foggy Christmas Eve arrived courtesy of a fog machine that had been brought in while no one was looking.

The fog was likely denser than anyone had anticipated, since they coughed and waved it aside. Eventually a jovial Santa appeared, striding through the fog and heading straight for Rudolph.

Abruptly the music ended and Santa dropped to one knee. "Rudolph, with your nose so bright, will you marry me tonight?"

19

What an awesome move. Quinn Sawyer had just become Seth's new hero.

The room grew silent. Not so much as a clink of silverware or a scrape of a chair.

Quinn glanced up. "Kendra?"

"I'm thinking."

A nervous titter ran through the crowd. Nobody wanted to see this go south. Seth certainly didn't. It was Christmas.

"Oh, of course I'll marry you, Quinn! I mean, Santa!" She laughed. "Wait, that would be weird. Santa's already married so he can't—"

"Santa can do whatever he wants." Quinn stood and pulled her into his arms. "He's the boss of Christmas." And he kissed her, causing her red nose to pop off and roll across the stage.

Relief gave the resulting shouts and cheers even more volume. Chaos reigned until Bryce once again stepped up to the mic and demanded order. "Is there a preacher in the house?"

"Godman!" someone cried out.

"I'm on it!" Warren Bennett, still in costume, pushed his way through the crowd and hopped up on stage, cape flapping. Then he glanced over at the happy couple. "They're still kissing."

"Yeah, I know," Bryce said. "We have to break that up."

Aunt Mo giggled. "Bryce doesn't realize the mic's still on."

Bryce stepped closer to the mic. "Yes, I do, Mrs. Stanislowski. I'm trying to shame my folks into giving up on the PDA so we can get this show on the road."

Quinn glanced up. "What did you say, son?"

"We have the preacher right here. If you two can postpone the lip-lock for a few minutes, we can get 'er done."

"Oh." He grinned and straightened his false beard. "Sorry about that. When Kendra hesitated, I took that as a sign that she needed more convincing. But I think we're ready, now." He glanced at her. "Are you good to go?"

Cheeks flushed, she nodded. "Yes."

The preacher glanced around. "How do you want to face? Toward the back of the stage or toward the audience?"

"Toward the audience," Aunt Kendra said. "My family is out there, and all of them have been asking if this would ever happen. I told them if it ever did, it would be a small private ceremony. They deserve an unobstructed view."

"This is really small, Mom!" Cody shouted. "You sure called it!"

That got a laugh.

"Blame it on me, son!" Quinn smiled at Aunt Kendra. "This was my cockamamie idea."

"And I love it." She wrapped an arm around his waist.

"Yeah?"

"Yeah." She kissed his cheek.

"Cool." Quinn raised his mitten-covered hand in Bryce's direction and they exchanged a high-five.

"Okay, you two," the preacher said. "Stand in the middle of the stage facing out. That's good. Do you have rings?"

Quinn shook his head. "That has to come later. It didn't feel right to choose rings without her and I wanted this to be a surprise."

"Nailed it. I never suspected." Aunt Kendra turned to the preacher. "Do you know the words by heart? Can you do this without your stuff?"

"I can."

"Then go."

Quinn heaved a sigh. "Thank God."

"I believe we all do," the preacher said. "Let's proceed."

Seth hadn't attended many weddings and had been involved in only one as a groomsman. None of them had been remotely like this—the groom in a Santa suit, the bride dressed as Rudolph minus the nose and the preacher in superhero spandex.

Oh, and not to mention that they were in a bar instead of a church, and the people in the room had accidentally become wedding guests. And it was the best wedding Seth had ever attended. The love between Aunt Kendra and Quinn enriched every word they said and every glance they exchanged.

As the preacher spoke the last words of the ceremony, the look that passed between Quinn and Aunt Kendra was pure gold. Seth tucked it deep in his heart. He wanted that, and now that they'd shown him it was possible, he wouldn't be satisfied with anything less.

The newlyweds were mobbed the minute the preacher finished, first by women in reindeer suits and then by everybody else. Seth ran interference for Zoe and Aunt Mo, who wanted a chance to dispense hugs and smiles. Once that was accomplished and he'd added his congratulations to the love fest surrounding Quinn and Aunt Kendra, he evaluated the situation.

Aunt Mo looked sleepy and Zoe's energy was flagging. She was pregnant, after all, and she'd admitted to not having the stamina she'd had before her pregnancy. He needed to take care of his ladies. "How about if I go fetch the car?"

They both looked relieved.

Aunt Mo nodded. "Good idea, son."

The party was still going strong when he retrieved his coat and hat and slipped out the front door. Bitter cold slapped him in the face. The wind had died down, but the temperature had dropped significantly.

What a day. He was alone on the street this time. No doubt many of those inside would party into the night. He would have, too, but getting Zoe and Aunt Mo home was more important.

He was shivering—*chitterin'* his da would have said—by the time he unlocked the SUV and climbed behind the wheel. The heater worked great, though, and the interior was toasty when he pulled up to the GG's front door. He left the motor running and hurried inside.

Four people stood waiting for him instead of two. His ma and da had joined Aunt Mo and Zoe and everyone had bundled up in coats and scarves.

"Slight change of plans," Aunt Mo said. "Hamish and Greer are dead on their feet but they hate to drag anyone else away so I said we'd take 'em home."

"Fine with me."

"It's out of your way, though." His ma held up her phone. "I just checked. The B&B's on the opposite side of town from the ranch."

Aunt Mo waved her hand dismissively. "This is Eagles Nest, not L.A. Nothing is that far away."

Seth ducked his head to hide a smile. Evidently when she was matchmaking, the distance was enormous. When she was offering his folks a ride, it shrank to nothing.

"We'll be takin' ye up on it, then," his da said. "Greer needs her rest."

"Aye, right." She gave him a playful nudge. "Ye do, too. We're not used to bein' oot on the skite."

"Then let's move out." Aunt Mo gestured toward the door. "Zoe, you take the front and I'll sit in back with Hamish and Greer."

"I'll sit in back, Aunt Mo. One of you can take the front."

Greer put an arm around Zoe. "Sit up front with Seth, *nighean*. We'll be takin' the back."

Seth blinked. He didn't know the meaning of the word she'd used, but it sounded like a term of endearment. And why was she coaxing Zoe to hang out with him in the front?

"Well, okay." Zoe's color was high.

Seth ushered them out the door and then circled the car getting everyone inside and buckled up. At last he slipped behind the wheel, closed his door and glanced in the rearview mirror. "Everybody set back there?"

"Well tidy, lad," his da said. "A bonnie lass to port and another to starboard."

Aunt Mo was small and logically belonged in the middle, but his da was taking one for the team by sitting between the women. With everyone wearing heavy coats, he was squished, and his long legs meant his knees nearly reached his chest, but he looked pleased with himself.

"Then we're off." Once he was on the road headed out of town, he checked on Zoe. "You warm enough?" He wasn't worried about the three packed tightly in the back seat.

"I'm just fine, thank you." She'd put her hood up for the trip out to the car, but she pushed it back and fluffed her hair with her fingers. She sent him a quick smile. "It'll be fun to see the ranch lit up at night."

"I was gobsmacked by all the lights," his ma said. "Kendra's decorations are pure barry."

"Aye," his da said. "A fairyland, it is. Even the barns have lights. Quinn said they do it every year."

Zoe twisted in her seat to glance back at them. "Do you put up lights at your house?"

"A little," his ma said. "Nothing like the ranch has."

Aunt Mo spoke up. "Have you had a good time so far?"

"Aye," his ma sighed happily. "'Tis grander than I ever dreamed of. And tonight, a surprise weddin'! How about that? Dinna she ken what he was up to?"

Seth made the turn onto the ranch road. "I don't think so. She wasn't acting any different when I was out there today. What do you think, da? Did she know in advance?"

"Nay," his da said. "She dinna ken. That Quinn, he's a sly one, bletherin' t'day like nothin' was goin' on."

Seth slowed down so he wouldn't jostle his passengers on the dirt road. "I thought it was an awesome idea." He glanced at Zoe. "What did you think?"

"He took a risk, for sure. I was worried there for a minute."

"Me, too," her aunt said. "It turned out to be exactly right, but I think that's because Quinn knows her well, maybe even better than she knows herself. She'd said she wanted a small private ceremony. Instead he gave her this."

"Even as a young lass, she was always one for surprises," his da said. "She loved it when Ian did somethin' unexpected. Ah, and here come the lights. Slow down a bit, son. Give us a look."

Letting up on the gas, Seth let the SUV glide in on the slight downslope toward the ranch house. "It does look like a fairyland, Da. Did I hear something about Aunt Kendra inviting you back for next year?"

"Aye. Could become a tradition."

"I hope it does." Eagles Nest was working its magic on his folks. Tonight it seemed to have touched Zoe, too. Three more days. Four nights. It wasn't much time. But he had his ma and Aunt Mo on his side. And it was Christmas.

20

Zoe tried to talk Aunt Mo into switching seats with her after they dropped off Hamish and Greer, but she was having none of it.

"It's like I'm being chauffeured," she proclaimed as Seth drove the SUV back down the ranch road. "Even better, chauffeured by my kids. I've envied my friends who get driven around by their adult children and children-in-law."

Zoe laughed. "If you want me to drive on our trips to town, just say the word. You can even sit in the back. I'll happily chauffeur you."

"I might start doing that. Not sitting in the back, though. That would be ridiculous. I'm doing it now because it does my heart good to see you two up there together."

Did it, now? Zoe went on alert. She'd always considered Aunt Mo an ally, but if she'd decided to start matchmaking, that wasn't cool.

Seth braked at the end of the dirt road and put on the turn signal. "Speaking of that, have you told Zoe about your housing plan for my return visits?"

"Not yet."

"What housing plan?" Zoe swiveled in her seat to look at her.

"I told him he's welcome to stay for free, assuming he'll be staying with you."

"We haven't talked about that." She glanced at Seth. "I'm sure Kendra would be glad to have you, and Wild Creek Ranch makes more sense. It'll also be free of charge."

"Trying to get rid of me?" He said it with a cute little smile.

"No, but the ranch is where the bulk of your family members will be. Wouldn't you rather—"

"I'd rather stay with you."

And spend his nights with her. The subtext sent heat through her veins, but prolonging their affair brought up some issues they needed to discuss before they blithely agreed to future sleeping arrangements.

"Your room isn't designed for a couple, though," Aunt Mo said. "If he'll be driving down quite a bit, it would make sense for you to move into his room for the rest of your stay."

A couple. Was that what they were, in her aunt's mind? If so, that merited a private discussion when Seth wasn't around. Instead she brought up a more practical objection. "His room is more expensive than mine. And more desirable. You said yourself mine is harder to rent because it's smaller and only has a double bed. That's one reason I haven't felt as guilty staying there." Her aunt made her living from the B&B, and the profit margins weren't huge as it was.

"I'll gladly pay for the bigger room." Seth reduced his speed as they cruised along a mostly deserted Main Street.

"We don't have to worry about that, now," Aunt Mo said. "Let's just plan on you staying at The Nesting Place when you come down and we can work out the details later."

"Fine with me. What do you think, Zoe?"

That her aunt's agenda was showing. Judging from her comments, she might be hoping that a romance with Seth would keep her favorite niece in Montana. "Aunt Mo's right. We don't have to decide anything right now."

"I agree."

Was he allowing himself to be carried away by the same fairy tale? He certainly wasn't objecting to her aunt's matchmaking efforts. She'd ask him when they were alone.

Except talking wasn't on the to do list once he shut the door to his room and twisted the lock. The pines outside his window blocked even the pale moonlight as velvet darkness closed around them. He didn't say a word and neither did she. He simply pulled her into his arms.

They could talk in the morning when she could focus on something other than... this.

She was as eager to get rid of her clothes as he was to ditch his. She threw back the covers and tumbled into bed. He dove in after her, kissing her lips, her throat, her breasts.

Writhing beneath him, she welcomed the fire that burned away everything but the powerful urge to love and be loved. He used his talented mouth to drive her insane, tracing a devastating path over each breast and down the valley between them. He crossed the swell of her belly and settled between her damp thighs.

His warm breath ramped up her anticipation. "I adore you," he murmured.

She gasped as he touched down and began to explore. His gentle, liquid caress sent heat flooding through her, sweeping away her inhibitions, carrying her to a place of reckless abandon. Her skin tingled. Her thighs quivered. And she begged for more.

He had more to give. He plunged deeper, used his tongue with deliberate intent, wound the spring tighter until she was panting, whimpering... and coming...

She grabbed a pillow to muffle her cries as he gifted her with wave upon wave of pleasure. As she arched into her release, he rose above her and sank his cock into her pulsing channel.

Two swift strokes and he shared the rocket ride with her, shuddering in the grip of his climax. His heaving chest brushed her skin as he gulped for air, but he kept his weight braced on his forearms. Gradually his ragged breathing eased.

Reaching up, she stroked his cheek. "You treat me so well."

"It's easy." Leaning down, he kissed her lightly on the mouth. "I wasn't even sure I should make love to you tonight. I'm afraid you're not getting enough sleep."

She smiled. "Let me worry about that."

"I meant to ask if you were too tired, but then I... just had to hold you and that was the end of the discussion."

"I wanted you as much as you wanted me."

"That makes me happy." He sighed. "But I guess it's time to face reality."

Her pulse rate jacked up. Had he been reading her mind? "It is?"

"We'd better set the alarm and get some sleep. Tomorrow will be another busy day."

"Oh." She relaxed.

"What did you think I meant?"

"That you were ready for a serious discussion."

"Not in the dead of night after making love."

"No."

"Have lunch with me tomorrow?"

"Sure."

"Great." He kissed her gently. "I'll set the alarm." He climbed out of bed and pulled the covers over her. "I'll be right back."

"Okay." She tugged a fluffy pillow under her head and snuggled into the passion-warmed sheets.

"Done." He slid under the covers and curled his body around hers, his arm draped over her, his hand cupping her baby bump. "Sleep tight."

"You, too." She snuggled against him, savoring his warmth. She'd clear the air of any misconceptions tomorrow.

* * *

She woke before the alarm was set to go off. Slipping quietly out of bed, she padded into her room, shivering.

She winced as she stepped on the cold tile in her bathroom. After turning on the shower, she waited for hot water and finally stepped under the spray. Ah, much better.

Was her belly slightly bigger? Eventually she wouldn't be able to see her toes. Her GYN had told her she could expect movement any day now.

When she turned off the water, she heard the shower going in Seth's bathroom, so he was up, too. He'd invited her for lunch but hadn't mentioned his plans for the morning. He might have something scheduled with his dad, since once they parted, an ocean would separate them instead of a four-hour drive.

She'd just finished dressing when Seth rapped on the connecting door. "Can I come in?"

"Sure."

"I won't hold you up." He walked into the room barefoot, wearing only his jeans, his hair still damp. "I wanted to let you know I won't be able to help you clean—"

"Hey, that was a one-time deal." She smiled. "Your situation has changed."

"I'd like to help the next two mornings, though."

"That's sweet, but I have it covered. You should spend the time with your dad. That's a priority." And she needed to keep her priorities front and center, firmly ignoring his considerable appeal.

"So are you. I'd help today, except I need to do some Christmas shopping."

"Getting some things for your folks?"

He nodded. "I brought some stuff for the people I expected to meet, but I'd like to add to it."

"Understandable. You might run into them shopping for you, though."

He laughed. "I hadn't thought of that. Thanks. I'll be on the lookout."

"Do you still have time for lunch?"

"Absolutely."

She took a breath. "Good, because we really do need some time to talk."

"I know." Closing the distance between them, he drew her into his arms, his gaze warm. "We'll work it out." He gave her a tender kiss and released her. "See you around noon."

"Okay." Work what out, exactly? Hadn't he been listening to her? Their relationship had an expiration date already set. "I'd better run." She gave him a quick smile and headed for the door.

21

Seth managed to find things for everyone on his list except Zoe. He'd have to come back in the morning and try again. Maybe if he had a private moment with Aunt Mo, she'd have suggestions.

He had a blast getting toys for the kids, Rhys and Noel. He paid attention to the age-appropriate labels, but that little Noel was such a pip that he thought she could handle some of the stuff intended for a two-year-old.

Then he went overboard in the newborn section. Rattles, teething rings, colorful soft balls for little hands to squeeze, a mobile for the crib— he loaded up.

The woman at the register smiled as she tallied his purchases. "I'm guessing someone's a new dad."

"Uh, no, not me. These are for a… a friend's baby."

"Lucky friend. You chose well."

"Thanks. It was fun." And he longed to be there to see the baby play with those things. Yesterday, as he'd watched Zane with Rhys and Cody with Noel, he'd had an epiphany. He wanted to be a dad. More specifically, he wanted to be a dad to Zoe's baby.

It was a crazy idea with a bunch of problems attached, so he hadn't said anything to her. Maybe he would during lunch. Or he might let it ride until the next time he came down.

On the drive back to the B&B he tried clearing the dirt from his windshield with the wash function and the wipers. Looked worse than ever. He wasn't taking Zoe to town with the windows like this. A quick glance at the clock on the dash confirmed he had enough time to wash them before noon.

She wasn't upstairs when he came back with his purchases, so after tucking them in his closet, he went looking for her. She was in the laundry room folding towels fresh out of the dryer. Warm, fragrant cotton and warm, fragrant woman.

She glanced up. "Hi. Aunt Mo said you were back. I'll be done in a few minutes."

"No rush. Can I help?"

"Thanks, but I'm almost done."

"Then I'll go out and wash my truck's windows. I can't stand the grime any longer."

"Okey-doke. See you soon." She gave him a sunny smile.

Her smile stayed with him as he went outside, pulled rags and a spray bottle from behind the passenger seat and started on the windshield.

He had a way better chance of being a dad figure in the baby's life if he offered to live in Milwaukee. But he couldn't live in Milwaukee.

Montana was his home. He belonged on a ranch, not in the city. He'd never questioned his mother's decision to stay here instead of following her beloved to Scotland. He would have made the same choice.

Which meant if he wanted a future with Zoe and her baby, he'd have to prove to her that Montana could be her home, too.

He finished a little before twelve and came back inside. She wasn't in the reception area. He glanced at the comfy-looking easy chairs he hadn't tried out. Unbuttoning his coat, he sat down in one.

That lasted less than a minute. His brain was a hamster wheel. He stood and started pacing. Would she ever consider staying here? She loved the yoga studio she'd worked so hard on and her folks lived back there, but there was a lot to love here, too.

"Bobby used to pace like that sometimes."

He turned toward the arched doorway into the breakfast room. "Just getting my exercise, Aunt Mo."

She came through the doorway into the reception area. "He never liked to admit something was bothering him, either."

He met her gaze. He could ask whether she thought Zoe might consider staying here. Nope. He'd talk it out with Zoe at lunch. Maybe. "I'd like to buy a gift for Zoe, something..."

"Romantic?"

"Yes, ma'am. But I've never seen her wear jewelry. I can't imagine her getting excited about flowers, even if I could find some."

"I agree about the flowers. She might wear a necklace if you gave it to her. Something delicate. When she was around eight she bought herself a cheap one with a heart that had her name engraved on it. She wore it constantly until it broke."

"Hm. I like that idea. I did notice the jewelry store on Main Street, but I didn't go in."

"The guy who owns it has been in business for at least fifty years, so you can trust whatever he recommends. And he does engraving."

"Thanks. I'll go in the morning."

"You two are plotting something," Zoe called out as she came down the stairs wearing a different top than she'd had on earlier.

Aunt Mo gave her a wave. "Of course we are, sweetheart. It's Christmas!"

"It is?" She pretended to be surprised. "I wondered what the fuss was about."

Seth got a look at the front of her sweater and grinned. "I guess it's pure coincidence that you're wearing a red sweater with Merry Christmoose on it."

"It was clean, so I thought what the heck?"

Aunt Mo gave a nod of approval. "Looks great on you. I know you were doubtful about the red."

"But Nicole convinced me last night. If she can wear red, so can I."

"I'm still humming the songs from the show," Aunt Mo said. "It was amaz—oops, I hear my phone. Have a good lunch." She hurried back to her private suite.

"That sweater would be a hit with the folks in my town. We're all about moose up there." He fetched her parka.

"I have yet to see one."

He helped her on with her coat and her sweet fragrance drifted his way. "Probably because they show up more in the spring."

"What time in the spring?"

"May, usually."

"I might be gone by then."

Yeah, that punched him in the gut. "When's the projected due date? I know it's in April, but—"

"The fifteenth, but I think she gave me that date so I'll be sure and get my taxes done way ahead of time."

"Are they complicated?" He opened the door and waited for her to go through.

"More so than an individual filing, but I love owning my own business so it comes with the territory." She flipped up her furry hood and zipped her jacket.

Moose and taxes. Not the main subjects on his mind and likely not on hers, either.

"Did you have any luck finding gifts for your family?"

"I did. Got my da a Western shirt and a vest, but I stuck with gift cards for Rory and Aleck. Just my luck I'd buy 'em something they already owned. Got my ma a small framed print of one of Quinn's scratchboards, two baby bobcats."

"She'll love that."

"I think so." He helped her into the truck.

"Nice job on the windows."

"Thanks." He closed the door, rounded the truck and climbed in. "Where do you want to go for lunch?"

"Have you been to Pie in the Sky yet?"

"No. Walked past it this morning. Got a whiff of good smells when someone came out the door."

"Then let's do that."

"Okay." He started the engine and backed out.

"I was thinking we'd talk over lunch, but maybe it's better to do it now instead of in a public place."

His breathing became wonky. "Okay." He shifted gears and gave the truck a little gas. Not much. He didn't want to be going very fast when he wasn't sure what she was about to say.

"I spoke to my aunt this morning about last night's conversation." She pulled back her hood and turned to look at him. "I asked her point-blank if she was playing matchmaker by encouraging you to stay here and offering you a free room."

He glanced over at her. Not a trace of amusement in her expression. "What did she say?"

"She admitted that played a part, but she also loves having you around. You remind her of Uncle Bobby. She fantasizes that if she'd had a son with him, he would be a lot like you."

"I'm honored she feels that way."

"It's very sweet, but… I asked her to lay off the matchmaking."

His chest tightened.

"She promised she would. I sensed your stepmother was also wanting to nudge us together last night."

"I noticed that, too."

"Maybe I'm misinterpreting, but you seem to be fine with these two women's efforts to pair us up."

He took a deep breath and stretched his arms against the steering wheel. "I guess I have my fantasies, too."

The truck's cab filled with deafening silence. At last she spoke. "Such as?"

He cleared his throat. "Yesterday I got a close-up view of what being a dad is like—the love in my da's voice when he talks with my brothers, the pride in Zane's eyes when he helps his son try to stand, the way Cody laughs when Noel does something cute. I want... I want that opportunity."

"Oh, Seth, I hope you're not—"

"Can you blame me? I lay my hand on your belly where a new life is growing and my gut instinct is to offer to be a part of that. To be that baby's daddy. To give him or her what I never had."

"Seth." She said his name softly. "Pull over."

He glanced in her direction. Her expression had softened and the light in her dark eyes hinted at an emotion that made his heart race. He eased on the brakes and pulled to the side of the dirt road.

She unfastened her seat belt, turned toward him and reached for his hand. "You should have everything you want." She held his hand tightly between both of hers. "But you can't have them with me. I'm going home in April. I grew up there, built a business I love, and now I'll raise my child there. My parents live there. For me, that's home."

He swallowed. "I know all that."

"I can't picture you moving to Milwaukee."

He shook his head. "Wouldn't work."

"Then you'll need to give up this fantasy."

"I don't know if I can."

"Would it be easier on you if you moved out to Wild Creek Ranch for the next few days? I'm sure Kendra would—"

"No."

"But—"

"Unless you want me to. I'll go if that's your preference."

"It's not. I just—"

"Then I'll keep my room at the B&B and hope you'll agree to share my bed until I leave."

"There's no way I could stay on the other side of those connecting doors."

"That makes two of us."

"But I'm worried about your return visits. You'll become even more invested and I don't want to give you false hope that—"

"If I get more invested, that's my problem, not yours. You've made your position perfectly clear." He managed a smile. "Let's just enjoy the magic of Christmas together." He'd need a sleigh full of magic to salvage this situation. A miracle or two wouldn't hurt, either.

22

The aroma of pastries baking and coffee brewing should have been comforting. Zoe wasn't comforted. Seth wanted what she couldn't give and that sucked. What had started out as a mutually satisfying escapade had become a gigantic problem.

She was stuck with it, too. They both were. Sending him to stay at Wild Creek when he wanted to be with her would only make the holiday more miserable for everyone.

For now, her best bet was to take his advice, forget about what happened after Christmas, and enjoy the magic of the holiday. The bakery hummed holiday cheer. Giant snowflakes and oversized Christmas ornaments hung from the ceiling, a Christmas tree stood in one corner and the windows featured a hand-painted scene from *The Nutcracker.*

Soon after their sandwiches and holiday-themed drinks arrived, an ENHS madrigal group came in and serenaded the customers. She couldn't ask for more festive surroundings.

She glanced out the window as shoppers loaded down with bags and boxes stopped to greet friends on the sidewalk. "I can see why my aunt chose to live here."

Seth took a drink of his peppermint-flavored coffee. "My ma and da really like it, too. They're seriously considering another trip next Christmas."

"That would be great for you and their sons."

"Sure would. Which reminds me. They want to take us to dinner tonight at the GG. Would you like to do that?"

"Just us? Not your brothers and their girlfriends?"

"They wanted them to come, but Aleck and Tansy are bartending tonight and Damaris's folks are flying in so she and Rory will be picking them up in Bozeman. Ma and Da invited your aunt, too. They made the reservation late enough that she can still supervise the B&B Happy Hour."

She hesitated. "I'd love to have dinner with your folks, but..." She lowered her voice. "Is that a good idea? I mean, since your ma seems to have her heart set on us becoming a couple?"

"There's no doubt about it. She said that on the phone when she called to ask about tonight."

"She came right out with it?"

"I was startled, too. I guess she could tell. She laughed and explained that she didn't mince words with Rory and Aleck and she intended to treat me the same." He smiled. "Kinda nice that she feels that way about me."

"How did you respond?"

"Told her just what you've told me."

She kept her voice low. "Then she knows I'm pregnant?"

"She already knew. She suspected it because you weren't having alcohol and she was even more convinced when you got misty-eyed during *When a Child Is Born.*"

"That doesn't seem like much to go on."

"I know, but then you and I looked at each other, like we shared a secret. At first she wondered if by some wild circumstance, the baby was mine. She asked Aunt Mo, who set her straight."

Her breath caught as a visceral reaction to *the baby was mine* tightened her womb. Not what she should wish for since that would make everything worse. But having Seth's baby would be... okay, not going there.

He gazed at her, his expression troubled. "You don't have to do this dinner thing if you think it'll create problems."

"No, I'd like to go. If your ma is used to straight talk, then there's no problem, is there?"

"I don't see one. I'll text them and say we can make it." He tapped on his phone and consulted the screen. "She must have been waiting for that text." He grinned and turned the phone toward her. "She does love her emojis."

"Yes, she does." Zoe counted ten, including big smiles, kisses, hearts, party hats and fireworks.

Seth tucked his phone away and picked up the remainder of his sandwich. "Since I have so many relatives in Eagles Nest and I really like the town, I'm thinking I might relocate here."

"I'm not all that surprised."

He finished chewing and swallowed. "I don't plan to say anything yet."

She smiled. "You just did."

"I know, but you're..." He took a deep breath. "Anyway, I'll take it slow, check out my prospects."

"Like what?"

"For starting my own business training foals. You gave me the idea."

"I did?"

"Not directly, but you started your business from scratch and made a go of it. I stayed at the Buckskin Ranch for years because my mom worked there as the cook, but now... that's not a factor."

"And you want to spread your wings." His horizons were expanding and she was thrilled for him.

He gazed at her. "Yeah, I do. It'll take a while to make the transition. Wouldn't be a good idea to start now. Not as many foals are born in the winter. It's a long-range plan, but it feels right."

She nodded. "I can tell. I think it's a great idea."

"Me, too." He finished his sandwich and pushed his empty plate aside. "Would you like anything else?"

"No, thanks. I should probably be getting back. I promised Danica I'd call in this afternoon. She interviewed a new instructor this morning and wants my opinion."

He pushed back his chair. "Then let's go." He looked at the check and laid some money on the table.

"How about we split this one?"

He smiled. "How about we don't? It's Christmas. Consider it a gift."

"All right. Thank you." She took her parka off the back of the chair and he helped her into it. "I didn't think to ask. How are your folks getting to the Guzzling Grizzly? Are we picking them up in Aunt Mo's SUV?"

"No, my da decided to rent a car. They're picking us up."

"Uh, okay. Has he ever driven on the right side of the road?"

"Absolutely. He used to live here in his late teens and early twenties. He'll be fine. It's like riding a bike. Muscle memory."

* * *

Five hours later, Zoe sat paralyzed in the back seat between Seth and Aunt Mo while Hamish McGavin accessed his muscle memory of driving on the right side of the road. Evidently that muscle had atrophied.

Greer didn't seem to notice. Or maybe she'd perfected her poker face during years of marriage to Hamish. In any case, she sounded like a woman making idle comments during a slow game of croquet.

She admonished him to *let up on the pedal a wee bit.* Or *mind the snow piled by the roadside.* She didn't scream once, not even when Hamish veered into the left lane and nearly smashed into an eighteen-wheeler head-on.

After that hair-raising moment, Seth offered to take over. "You know what, Da? I'm in a driving mood tonight. How about trading places with me so you can relax and enjoy the ride?"

"I *am* enjoyin' the ride, lad! Takes me back, it does. Wish this vehicle had a standard transmission. I used to love poppin' the clutch and—"

"Da! Watch out for the—" Seth gasped. "Mailbox."

The SUV passed within an inch of a rural mailbox. It wiggled from the whoosh of air sweeping past.

"Ah, we're nearin' the edge of town." Hamish braked hard enough to throw each of them against their seat belts. "Might want t'take it easy. Watch for the fuzz."

Greer glanced at him, looking uneasy for the first time. "The *fuzz*?"

He waved a hand. "American word. The police to you, lass." He stopped driving like a contestant in the Grand Prix and overcorrected until he was creeping down Main Street at the pace of a float in the Rose Bowl Parade.

Cars piled up behind them, which was saying something. Zoe had never seen bumper-to-bumper traffic in Eagles Nest. Hamish managed to create it.

"You can go a little faster, Da." Seth was behind the driver's seat, a good coaching position if he'd been allowed to do any coaching. "The speed limit's twenty-five."

"What's that in kilometers? I used t'know this cold, but it's been a few years."

"I don't know, but it doesn't matter. Just go fast enough to hit twenty-five on the speedometer."

"Is that why I have this line of cars followin'? I'm goin' too slow?"

"That's the situation, Da."

"Then why dinna you say so?" He tromped on the gas and the tires squeaked as he peeled out.

Aunt Mo had reached her limit. "Hamish, you're going to kill us all. Pull over and I'll drive."

"Dinna fash yerself, bonnie lass." He hung a sharp left against oncoming traffic into the parking lot of the Guzzling Grizzly. The SUV screeched to a stop inches from the front door. "We've arrived."

Greer patted him on the shoulder. "Well done, *leannan*."

As Seth helped Zoe out, he put his mouth next to her ear. "I'll drive us back. He'll want to have a few drinks. That should do it."

She nodded. "Good plan."

A country band provided the music as they walked in. Aunt Mo had checked online and informed them Nicole and Bryce were taking a much-needed break before their Christmas Eve performance.

The coat check was in operation again tonight. Once they'd dispatched with coats and hats, Jenny showed them to a round table a row back from the dance floor.

Zoe took the chair Seth pulled out for her. Then he seated his stepmother on his other side and Hamish helped Aunt Mo into a chair on Zoe's left.

As Jenny passed out menus, she grinned at Seth. "I should've figured out you were related to this bunch the first time I laid eyes on you."

"But you weren't expecting it."

"Never occurred to me. Had us buzzing around here, that's for sure." She pulled out her electronic order pad and took their drink orders. "I've been told your drinks will be delivered personally by the bartender," she said with a wink before she left.

Zoe glanced toward the bar where Aleck and Tansy worked side-by-side. Her aunt's intel was that Seth's brother had given up a thriving law practice in Scotland to move to Eagles Nest and start over. "How close is Aleck to getting certified to practice law here?"

"Och, he's just gettin' started," Hamish said. "Could be years. He dunna care how long it takes if he can be with that bonnie lass."

"Aye, some things are worth waitin' for." Greer settled her reading glasses on her nose and picked up her menu. "Well tidy scran here. I dunna ken what to order."

"Scran?" Aunt Mo lifted her eyebrows. "Is that the word for food?"

Greer nodded. "'Tis."

"I'll add it to my vocabulary. By the time I come over to visit, I'll be fluent."

"Ye are comin' t'see us?" Greer peered at her over the glasses. "When?"

"Whenever the rest are going."

"The rest?"

"I guess you didn't hear. There's a plan afoot to go as a group. I'm not sure who's in charge of it, but—"

"I heard it from Trevor," Seth said. "He called it *Montana McGavins invade Scotland.* Asked if I wanted in. I told him absolutely."

Greer beamed. "That's grand! How about this summer, then? Somethin' t'look forward to. I hate the thought of leavin', but if ye are comin', I can bear it."

"We'll ask Kendra, lass."

"Aye, we'll do that." Greer turned to Zoe. "Ye will come?"

"To Scotland? Oh, I... well, probably not if it's this summer."

"Ah, the wee bairn. But they travel easier when they're young."

"Maybe, but there's the yoga studio. I doubt—"

"I'd like to talk to ye about that."

"My studio?"

"Aye."

"She has a bonnie plan, lass. Can't wait for ye t'hear it. She—"

"Lads and lasses, I bid you welcome to our humble tavern." Aleck arrived, a loaded tray held aloft and balanced expertly on one hand. He gestured to the tray. "Behold, three frosty orders of McGavin's Pale Ale, aka nectar of the gods, presented in our signature Guzzling Grizzly mugs, a glass of dry red in a signature goblet for the discriminatin' proprietor of The Nesting Place, and one frosty sarsaparilla for bonnie Zoe, also presented in a signature GG mug."

Hamish chuckled. "'Tis what happens when a solicitor takes up bartendin'. He canna just serve the drinks."

"Where's the fun in that?" Aleck served everyone except Zoe. Then he swept a bow in her direction while handing over the sarsaparilla. "For the sweet lady who aided my brother in his noble quest. I dinna get the chance to thank you last night so I'm doin' it now."

She blushed. "You're welcome, but I didn't really—"

"Yes, she did." Seth stood and held out his hand to Aleck. "Well done. She's been a huge help."

Aleck gripped his hand. "And we're all grateful. Just to give you fair warnin', Rory and I are plottin' and schemin' to get you to move down here."

"Is that so?" Seth grinned.

"We'll blether about it later. Maybe on Christmas Day." He spun the tray on one finger before flashing a smile at his folks. "Signal when you need another round." He turned and headed back to his duties.

Greer rolled her eyes. "I dinna ken he'd enjoy tendin' bar so much."

"The lad's in love. He's enjoyin' everythin' right now." Hamish picked up his mug. "Followin' Aleck's fine example, let us raise a glass to Zoe, who lit the way through the darkness, guiding our Seth back to us."

Her cheeks warmed.

Greer held up her mug. "To Zoe. *Slainte.*"

Aunt Mo raised her mug, too. "Is that a toasting word?"

"Aye," Greer said. "It means *health*, which I know we all wish for Zoe."

"Absolutely." Aunt Mo looked over at Zoe. "*Slainte*, sweetheart."

"Thank you."

Next to her, Seth raised his mug and held her gaze. "*Slainte*, Zoe." Goodwill shone in his eyes.

She smiled because all four people clearly wished her well. Aleck, too. But all the good wishes in the world wouldn't change the facts. In four months, she'd be gone.

23

Seth nursed his drink because it would have to last him. He'd be the designated driver on the way home. Much as he loved his da, the guy was a danger behind the wheel.

It was a problem easily corrected. He'd handle the situation tonight and maybe he and his da would have a chance in the next two days to go out on a lonely country road and practice. Some father and son time would be good.

Their server took their food order and brought complimentary munchies. The band played a Western version of *Danny Boy* because they'd heard there was a Scottish clan chief in the house. Seth got a kick out of his dad's pleased reaction. It was good to be a McGavin.

Best of all, Zoe looked happy. Her brown eyes sparkled as she talked with his da about growing up on a sheep farm outside of Eagles Nest.

Not surprisingly, a sheep farm in an area populated by wolves hadn't worked out for his grandparents. His Scottish grandparents had relocated and were still thriving on the far side of the Atlantic. Hard to believe. Yeah, he had to get over there and meet them.

Then the conversation shifted to Zoe's yoga studio. She became even more animated as she described her program, her instructors and her students.

"And you built it from the ground up?" His ma sounded impressed.

"I did. I'm proud of that."

"Must be fun, havin' that challenge."

"Scary at times, but... yeah, fun."

His ma nodded in understanding. "If it's a goin' concern, might fetch a gud price. Or a steady income as the buyer pays it off."

The other shoe had dropped. Seth should have seen it coming. Cagey, those two.

Zoe's eyes widened, but instead of calling the idea crazy, she laughed. "Doesn't matter because I'm not selling it."

"Thought ye'd say that. But afore ye dismiss the idea, will ye let me speak?"

"Go ahead. You won't change my mind, though."

"There's no yoga studio here and I canna imagine a better place to raise a wee bairn."

"It's the *perfect* place." Aunt Mo put her arm around Zoe. "And I'm the quintessential babysitter. I'm there all the time."

Zoe glanced at her. "Did you know about this idea?"

"I didn't, but wow, do I love it." She gave Zoe's shoulder a squeeze. "You could have free lodging and a live-in sitter while you got your studio up and running."

Zoe glanced over at Seth. "Did you know about any of this?"

"I did not." And he couldn't tell from Zoe's reaction whether his ma had just sunk him or saved him.

She faced his ma again. "I give you points for ingenuity, but I have my game plan for supporting my child. You're asking me to abandon that plan and build a new business in conjunction with adjusting to having a newborn."

"Aye, I grant ye that. One more point to make and I'll be done. We blethered with Kendra this mornin'. She texted her Whine and Cheese Club friends. They loved the idea."

"That's only six women."

"Six of the most influential women in town." Aunt Mo drained her wine glass. "If you have their support, you're almost guaranteed to make it. I think this calls for another round."

"Aye." His da stood. "I'll go tell Aleck—"

Seth got up. "That's okay, Da. I'll fetch it."

"Thank you, son." He sat down. "I dunna want to miss any of this."

Seth was more than willing to miss all of it. Zoe was being polite, but she would dig in her heels any minute now. Then she'd be more determined than ever to follow her original plan.

He might have little to no chance to influence her on that score after she dealt with his ma and Aunt Mo. But he hadn't totally abandoned the field, either.

He'd figured time was on his side and he'd hoped to use every visit to subtly make his case that her baby needed a father. His ma, by focusing on the economic picture, might have sabotaged that effort.

He approached the bar and Aleck gave him a friendly smile. Someday they'd have the kind of relationship that would allow them to lean on each other in times of stress. But that didn't exist yet and now wouldn't be the time for a heart-to-heart, anyway.

"What can I get you, bro?"

"A refill for everyone but me, please. I'm the designated driver."

"Got it." He grabbed mugs for the beer. "Da will appreciate that. I heard he rented a car."

"And he thinks he's still a twenty-two-year-old in a hot rod. The drive over was hairy."

"It was?" Aleck set the beer mugs on a tray. "Even though he learned to drive over here?"

"That was more than thirty years ago. To say he's rusty is an understatement."

"Full disclosure." He poured Aunt Mo's red wine and added it to the tray. "He's not that great a driver in Scotland, either."

"Oh. I was thinking it was just the other-side-of-the-road thing."

"Nay. I was hopin' he'd be cautious since he's dealin' with a different paradigm, but evidently not."

"Cautious is not a word I'd use to describe his driving habits."

"Cautious is not a word I'd use to describe him, period." He gazed at Seth. "Our father is an impulsive man. That's where Rory gets it."

Our father. Nice to hear. "So you inherited his coloring and Rory got his disposition?"

"Pretty much." He put Zoe's sarsaparilla on the tray. "If I'm readin' you right, you're like me. You look like him but you act more like your mother."

"To a point, you're right. But she wasn't willing to take risks to find what she wanted. I am, so maybe I have some of Da's impulsive behavior, after all."

"That's actually good news, because Rory and I have plans for you."

"The ones we'll *blether* about on Christmas Day?"

Aleck pointed a finger at him. "Aye. Keep talkin' like that and we'll turn you into a Scotsman, yet."

"That's doubtful. I'm a hundred percent Montana cowboy."

"That's where you're wrong. You're fifty percent clan chief. Don't fight it, bro."

Seth laughed. "Okay. What do I owe you for these?"

"Nothing. I'm covering it. My folks."

"Mine, too." Seth pulled out his wallet. "I'll split it with you."

Aleck eyed him with a smile. "Spoken like a McGavin. I'll take that offer."

Seth got square with Aleck and carried the tray back to the table. "Don't expect me to balance this one handed or twirl it on my finger. But I have your drinks."

"Thanks, son." His da smiled. "We've tabled the yoga studio discussion for the time bein'."

Zoe had put her foot down. "I see." He didn't look at her. Instead he made himself very busy passing out the drinks. Luckily their food showed up within seconds of the time he sat down, so there was no lag in the action.

After dinner, his ma and da wanted to enjoy the dancing. He and his da took turns partnering two women at once. It should have been fun and sometimes it was, but he longed to take Zoe out on the floor alone. They needed some one-on-one time.

When his folks and Aunt Mo announced that they'd had enough, his ma insisted he should take Zoe out for one last dance before they went home. At last he had his chance. He gathered her into his arms as the band played a two-step that could be danced fast or slow. He chose slow.

"I know what you're thinking," she murmured.

"Do you?" Her body against his stole his breath.

"That I'm upset because your stepmother is trying to keep me in Montana for your sake."

"Are you?"

"I can't be upset with Greer. She has mothering instincts. She knows you care for me and she wants to help."

"And because I... care for you, I want you to ignore her suggestion."

She glanced up at him. "You do? But wouldn't you want—"

"You know I do. But you're right. Tackling a new business venture while dealing with a newborn is asking too much."

"Like Aunt Mo said," she murmured, "you're a good man."

"Thanks." But holding her short-circuited his brain. He'd become a heat-seeking missile and she was the target. Pitiful.

"You don't want to discuss this anymore, do you?"

"No, ma'am. I'm at a disadvantage."

"Why?"

"When I get this close to you, my powers of reason disappear. I just want to make love to you. Evidently you don't have that problem."

"I do sometimes. Not always."

"That's depressing."

"Okay, *most* of the time I just want to get naked with you. But not when we're having a night out with your folks and Aunt Mo."

He sighed. "I wish I could say the same."

"It's okay. Once we get back to your room, we'll talk."

"Not if I can help it." He wasn't making sense and he didn't care. Chances were very good he'd eventually have to give her up, and she was everything he'd ever wanted.

She was heading to Milwaukee just like his da had flown to Scotland. And like his mother, he wouldn't follow her to a place that didn't suit him. In that case, he might as well let his body have its way while she was still within reach. The party would end soon enough.

"Then we'll make love first and then talk."

"Sure." So far talking with her hadn't yielded any results. No reason they should this time, either. But if they made love first, at least he'd have that.

24

"I'm glad you could go tonight, Aunt Mo." Zoe kept her voice down as she and her aunt slipped quietly into the B&B's fairy-lit reception area. Seth came in behind them and locked up.

"I was thrilled to be included." Her aunt took off her coat and hung it by the door. "That's two dinners out in a row. I'll get spoiled."

"Not you." Zoe hung her parka next to Aunt Mo's wool coat and turned to her. "You're incredibly giving. And your willingness to care for my child is... above and beyond. I'll never forget the generosity of that offer."

"I wouldn't have made it if I didn't want to." She glanced at Seth. "Thanks for being the designated driver."

"We couldn't risk another ride like that first one." He took off his Stetson and ran his fingers through his hair. "When I take the car back tomorrow, I'll try to work in a driving lesson."

"Excellent strategy." Aunt Mo's gaze swung back to Zoe. "Regarding my offer of childcare, sweetheart, I would love having the chance to watch over your baby. But I understand why you want to stick with your original plan."

"You're the best, Aunt Mo."

"I am pretty awesome." She smothered a yawn. "And now I'm toddling off to bed. See you in the morning."

"Sweet dreams." She gave her aunt a hug and watched her walk back to her private quarters. "I didn't realize how much she's looking forward to the baby."

"Yeah."

She glanced up at him. "Coming here for the duration seemed like such a simple solution. Looks like I miscalculated."

His expression softened. "Regrets?"

"Not really. If I hadn't felt the need to escape Milwaukee, I wouldn't have met you."

"I hadn't thought of that."

"Oh, I have. There were a lot of moving parts. Change one thing and we wouldn't be standing here wondering how to handle this situation we've created."

The corners of his mouth tilted up. "We could start by going upstairs. And since people are sleeping..." He backed up to Aunt Mo's desk, leaned against it and pulled off his boots.

"Right." She moved over to the stairs, sat down and took hers off, too. "I like to think I wouldn't have forgotten, but I'm a wee bit distracted tonight." Boots in hand, she started up the stairs.

He followed, his footsteps silent except when the old wood creaked under his weight. "Just so you know, I'd rather not have any deep discussions tonight."

"Would you rather submerge ourselves in a fantasy world of passion and pleasure?"

"Sounds good."

"Then let's do that." She scampered up the stairs. Before she'd made it to his door, he caught up with her.

Wrapping an arm around her waist, he tugged her against his aroused body. His voice rumbled in her ear. "Let's turn on the lights before we start. I want to be able to see you."

"By all means turn on some lights." Heat sluiced through her. "While you do that, I'll make good use of my time."

He released her with a groan. "You drive me insane." He fumbled with the key and swore softly. "Can't even get in the stupid room." Jabbing the key in the lock, he twisted it impatiently and shoved open the door. "After you."

His excitement fueled hers. Trembling, she stepped into the room and began stripping off her clothes.

He turned on the lamp on the far side of the bed as she unhooked her bra and tossed it aside. He came around the bed and switched on the other lamp.

Sliding out of her panties, she threw back the covers, shivering from a combination of cold air and hot desire. "I'm getting in. I'm freezing."

"I have a solution for that condition."

"Let's see it."

"Glad to oblige." Snaps popped as he ripped open his shirt, Superman style. Yanking it from the waistband of his jeans, he took it off and tossed it aside. A snug white T-shirt that molded to his pecs was the next to go. Reaching behind his back, he pulled it over his head and let it fly. "This top section will help insulate you from the cold."

"Nice." Her throat tightened. He was so beautiful, inside and out. But she'd have to give him up.

His chest heaved as he unbuckled his belt. "This bottom section is critical to the warming function. It contains the heating element." His belt buckle rattled as he shoved down his jeans and briefs. "Think that'll work with your equipment?"

"It should." She ached for him. It wasn't a mild, easy-to-ignore ache, either. More like a demand from her core. "How about a demo?"

"Happy to provide one. Scoot on over and I'll—"

"I'm staying put. I've warmed up this section of the sheets."

"Then I guess I'll skip the preliminary testing."

"Good idea." She lifted the covers. Cool air tickled her damp inner thighs as she opened them. "I'm ready for you to hook up the heating element."

His breath caught. "Lady, you have top-of-the-line equipment. This will be a short demo."

"I don't care. I'm already sold on your product. Give it to me." She gulped. "Please."

"Yes, ma'am." Grasping the covers, he drew them around his shoulders as he moved over her. "Feel free to handle it and get familiar with—" He sucked in a breath as she wrapped her hand around his cock and squeezed gently. "On second thought, you might want to hold off."

"But I like how it feels in my hand."

"I like how your hand feels on my... element." His voice grew hoarse. "You're about to cause an overload."

"Then maybe we should find out how it fits. Come closer."

"Can't help it. You're in control." His breathing roughened as he lowered his hips.

She guided him to her entrance and lifted to meet him, her gaze fastened on his. "I like this part."

"I love this part." He gulped. "Let go. I've got this."

"Okay." She relinquished her hold, slid her hands up his lightly furred chest and gripped his shoulders.

He pushed home and held himself there, his eyes filled with intense emotion. "I love you, Zoe. You and that sweet baby."

She forgot to breathe. Digging her fingers into his broad shoulders, she forced air into her lungs.

His smile was tender. "Didn't expect that, did you?"

She shook her head and dragged in more air.

"I didn't... I didn't expect to say it." His throat moved in a slow swallow. "Not now, anyway. But I need to tell you... in case... I never get another—"

She pressed her fingers to his lips. "Don't." Trailing her fingers over his mouth, she caressed his cheek. "Let's just focus on right now."

"And right now, I. Love. You. Nothing will change that."

"Oh, Seth." Her heart thudded hard and breathing hurt like the devil. "That's such a big thing to say."

"It's such a big thing to feel." He began moving, stroking slowly. "I wondered if I'd recognize it when it came along. Turned out to be easy."

Pressure built behind her eyes. "I don't want you to get hurt."

"That's good." He settled in, thrusting with more deliberate intent. "I'd like to skip that, if possible."

"But there's so much we can't..."

"Resolve? I know. But none of it has anything to do with me loving you. That's a constant no matter what. That's why I told you." Leaning down, he kissed her gently. Then he drew back a fraction, his breath warm on her face. "Please remember it."

She squeezed her eyes shut to hold back the tears. "I could never forget."

"That's good, too." He brushed his mouth over hers. "I wanted to say it when I had your undivided attention."

"You have it."

"Great." He peppered her face with light kisses. "Then what do you say we dive into that fantasy world of passion and pleasure you mentioned on the way up here?"

Her breath hitched. He wanted to lighten the mood and end the evening on a high note.

Sweet of him to try, even if the effort was doomed. "Sure."

"Hang on."

She wrapped her arms around his back and hooked her legs around his. "All right. I'm buckled in."

"Then here we go."

She gasped as he launched into a rapid pace that had her climaxing in seconds. He slowed briefly, then took her up again on a rocket ride that left her breathless. Her world exploded a second time.

Breathing hard, he eased her back to the mattress. "One more... slower, though."

She sucked in air. "I... can't..."

"Sure you can." He rocked back and forth. "We'll come together this time." He licked a drop of sweat from the hollow of her throat. "Warm enough?"

"I'm a furnace."

"Yeah, you are." His gaze searched hers. "It's fun stoking you up."

She combed a damp lock of hair from his forehead. "You're incredible, Seth Turner."

"Thank you, ma'am." He shifted his angle. "One more time, pretty lady."

Sure enough, he brought her to the edge again.

As she gripped his muscled arms, he took her over the brink and followed her there, gasping those three words, words that changed everything.

And nothing.

25

The words were out. Seth couldn't take them back and didn't want to. But he and Zoe needed another discussion now that he'd introduced love into the equation. His declaration had likely added pressure to an already touchy situation.

But they both fell asleep immediately after their epic lovemaking and didn't wake up until the alarm went off in the morning.

He helped with breakfast and afterward let her know he was returning the rental to his da. ""I can't say when I'll be back. There's a Christmas Eve service at Godman's church I'd like to attend, if you would be interested in—"

"Godman? Is that what people are calling him, now?"

"That's what Da said. This last talent show performance clinched it. Would you like to go?"

"I'd love to."

"How about Aunt Mo?"

"She plans to have a quiet night at home, preparing the goody bags she leaves on everyone's doorknob. It's her Secret Santa thing and she loves it. She's shortened Happy Hour since it's Christmas Eve."

"She's coming to Wild Creek with us tomorrow, I hope."

"That's another reason she wants to stay home. She's making a casserole to take. She's looking forward to going over there."

"Good. By the way, I thought I'd get something quick for dinner tonight. I can bring you a burger or a pizza if you'd like that."

She smiled. "What will you be driving?"

"Oh. Right. I'll see if someone can drop me off here."

"Your father?"

He grimaced. "Maybe I'll talk him into letting me use the rental for a while. Whatever happens, I'll make it back here and I can bring food."

"What time is the service?"

"Seven-thirty."

"My folks are supposed to call around six our time. Why don't you grab something for yourself and I'll have supper with Aunt Mo while we talk to my parents?"

He nodded. "Does seven work?"

"Perfect. See you then."

He gave her a quick kiss and vamoosed out of there. Until they could be alone with time to talk, the less said the better.

He wouldn't mind a little advice, though. As luck would have it, his da had appointed himself a dispenser of wisdom. The man's driving was atrocious but he was a kind and generous soul. He'd also wrestled with a similar problem years ago.

Considerably fewer trucks sat in the parking area near the ranch house than when he'd been here the last time. He added the white SUV to the lineup and headed for the front door. Laughter came from inside as he mounted the steps.

Quinn opened the door before he had a chance to knock. "Thought I saw you drive up when I went to get more coffee. Come on in. We were just discussing the honeymoon. I'm having a hard time talking your Aunt Kendra into it."

"Not surprised." Seth stepped through the door and took off his hat. Cozy setup. His folks and Kendra lounged by a crackling fire. The décor was the same as when he'd been here before—a large Christmas tree by the front window, the mantle decorated with pine boughs and pinecones. But the decorations hadn't registered so clearly in the midst of an emotional few hours with his family.

Quinn offered him coffee and he politely refused. "Da and I have business in town, don't we, Da?"

"Aye, lad." His father picked up his coffee mug. "I'll just put this in the dishwasher. Then we'll be off."

Aunt Kendra smiled. "I love that he does that. Ian never left his dirty dishes around, either. I was too young to appreciate the job their mother did raising those boys, but I do, now."

"If this grand Montana McGavin invasion materializes," his ma said, "you can thank her in person this summer."

"It will materialize." Aunt Kendra had a gleam in her eye as she turned to Quinn. "And it's ridiculous to jet off to Fiji next month if we're going to Scotland in June."

"Different trips for different purposes." Quinn flashed her a grin. "I happen to know you own a bikini, and I want to see you wearing it on a tropical beach far from the snows of a Montana winter."

Kendra blushed. "You're not allowed to mention that bikini."

"I promise I'll never bring it up again if you'll agree to fly off to the South Pacific with me."

"Och, Kendra!" His ma flapped her hand in Kendra's direction. "Go on the tropical honeymoon with your lovely husband, for God's sake. It'll be pure barry and ye can tell us all about it in June."

Aunt Kendra laughed. "Am I being a stick in the mud?"

"Aye, and from what I hear from your Whine and Cheese ladies, that's not like ye."

Aunt Kendra gazed at her new husband. "I'll go."

"*Yes.*" Quinn pumped his fist. "Thank you, Greer." He rounded the couch and gave her a kiss on the cheek.

"What did I miss?" His da came out of the kitchen.

"Your wife convinced my wife to go on the damn honeymoon." Quinn shoved his hands in his pockets, rocked back on his heels and beamed at the group. "Which is a good thing, because I already bought the tickets."

"Quinn!"

He shrugged, clearly unrepentant. "It was a smokin' deal."

She rolled her eyes. "I'll *deal* with you later, buster."

"I hope so."

And that was the kind of playful, loving relationship Seth wanted with Zoe. He glanced at his da. "Ready?"

"After you, lad." He closed the door behind him and they started for the SUV. "They get on well, Kendra and Quinn."

"Like you and ma."

"Aye, but we've been rubbin' along for years. Kendra and Quinn are new at this. But 'tis like they've been at it much longer."

"I feel like that with Zoe."

"Ye do seem suited to each other." He held out his hand. "I need the keys."

Seth fished them out of his pocket. "Da, things got a little wild on the road last night. I—"

"Aye, right. Acted like a right chancer, dinna I?"

"You gave us a few scares."

"I'll not scare ye on this trip, lad."

"Good." He climbed in the passenger seat and buckled up.

His da got behind the wheel, put the key in the ignition and started the engine.

"Da? Your seatbelt?"

"Oh." He fastened the buckle, put the SUV in reverse, and spit gravel as he tromped on the gas. "See that? This thing has power!"

"Which is the point I want to make. It's heavy, so if you hit something going fast, you could do major damage."

"Dunna worry. I won't hit anythin'." He swung the SUV around, tromped on the gas again and the vehicle leaped forward.

"Now, see, that's what I'm talking ab—"

"I dunna think my wee car responds this quick. Good thing it's daylight. Last night I could barely see anythin'." He veered toward the ranch road and propelled the SUV in that direction at breakneck speed, hitting every bump.

"Slow down, Da!"

He turned and grinned. "Where's your spirit of adventure, lad?"

"I have something important to talk to you about! Pull over, okay?"

"Aye, if we must." He swerved to the wrong side of the road and ended up in a slush-filled ditch at a thirty-degree angle. "This dinna feel right. D'ye think we're stuck, then?"

Seth glanced at him and fought the urge to laugh. "Yeah, Da, I think we're stuck."

"We hardly went a kilometer!"

"I know." He grinned. "Quinn will have to pull your ass out of this ditch."

"Aye." He sighed. "Ye know what they say. *Bad decisions make good stories.*"

"Who says that?"

"I dunna ken. Some eejit." He let out a muffled snort. "I'd better text Quinn."

"Yep. Get it over with. Face the music." He met his da's gaze and they both cracked up.

His da wiped his eyes. "'Tis not funny, lad." Then he burst out laughing again. "Textin' Quinn." His phone pinged. "What's *WTF*?"

Seth lost it. Eventually he had enough breath to explain and then his da lost it.

His da's phone pinged again. "He's comin'. What was so important to talk to me about?"

"Zoe. She's determined to go back home and raise that baby alone. I don't want her to leave and I don't want to think of that little kid growing up without a dad, especially when I'm... when I want so much to..." As he ground to a halt, breathing hard, he glanced at his father. "What would you do?"

"Would ye go to this place—Milwaukee?"

He shook his head. "My life is here. My work with foals is here. It's all I've ever wanted to do. Besides, I can't imagine walking outside and not seeing mountains."

"Yer mother felt the same about Montana. Does Zoe love Milwaukee, then?"

"She was born there so I'm sure she does love things about it and her folks are there. She definitely loves her yoga studio."

"She dinna like the idea of openin' a new one here?"

"No. She believes in making a plan and following the plan. I've tried to explain that it can be a very lonely life for a kid with one parent and no siblings. Hard on the single parent, too. But... I don't think she gets it."

"Aye. She has no experience." His da's gaze shifted to the snow-covered landscape. "M'heart aches fer ye and your mother. But she made the choice. I dinna have a say in it." He sighed. "The truth of it is, ye dunna have one with this wee bairn, either."

"I know. And that's frustrating as hell."

"Ye love her?"

"I do."

His da's gaze was steady. "Does she ken ye love her?"

"I told her last night."

"Does she love ye back?"

"She didn't say so, but... I think, maybe."

"There's the key, lad. She must love ye back." His gaze was direct. "Warts and all."

26

A few minutes before seven, Zoe hurried upstairs to put on another of the holiday tops her mother had sent a couple of weeks ago. They fit loosely and disguised her baby bump, at least for now.

She rolled up the yoga mat she'd left out when she'd had to rush down in time to join Aunt Mo for her folks' call. She'd grabbed thirty minutes beforehand to do some stretching.

At seven she descended the stairs just as Seth came through the front door, his cheeks ruddy from the cold and his Stetson at a jaunty angle.

He glanced up at her and smiled.

She paused and gripped the railing, captured by the warmth in his green eyes. He loved her. And, heaven help her, she loved him. Which meant ending this fantasy before things got really out of hand. She just had to decide when to do it.

He grabbed her parka off the hook and met her at the bottom of the stairs. "We need to get a move on. I left my folks in the SUV with the motor running."

"They didn't want to come in and see the place?"

"They would have loved to, but Aunt Kendra warned me that the church fills up fast on Christmas Eve." He helped her into her parka.

"Okay. Just let me tell my aunt we're leaving." She hurried over to the arched door leading into the breakfast room. "I'm taking off, Aunt Mo!"

"Have fun, sweetheart!" she called back.

"Thanks!" Oh, yeah. Fun times. Not. She zipped her parka on her way back to Seth. He opened the door and she hurried through it. The SUV sat at the end of the walkway, a steady stream of exhaust coming from the tailpipe. "Are you in permanent possession of the rental?"

"Yes, ma'am." He laughed. "Da ran us into a ditch only a few yards down the ranch road. Quinn had to tow us out."

"Oh, dear." His laughter hurt her soul. She pulled up her hood. "Was he embarrassed?"

"Maybe a little, but mostly he thought it was funny. Quinn will never let him live it down, but da can take it. He gave me the keys and said I could keep the SUV until I left on the twenty-sixth. I can drive you and Aunt Mo over to Wild Creek Ranch tomorrow."

Her stomach pitched. If she ended things tonight or tomorrow, she'd put a big hole in his Christmas. Just because hers was already ruined didn't mean his had to be, too. "I'm just glad he gave up driving, at least for this trip."

"Me, too." He opened the front passenger door and gave her a hand in.

She turned and greeted his folks before buckling up. "How was your day?"

Hamish chuckled. "You mean other than landin' in a ditch and havin' to be hauled out by my host?"

"Seth mentioned that."

"Fancies himself Mario Andretti, he does," Greer muttered.

"Ah, my bonnie lass. Ye love a man with adventure in his soul."

She snorted. "And a head full o' mince."

"Ye love that, too."

Zoe glanced in the rearview mirror and caught Hamish leaning over to kiss Greer on the cheek and murmur something in her ear. She gave him a playful shove.

Seth grinned. "You two behave yourselves back there." Clearly he was having the time of his life with Greer and Hamish in town.

Zoe looked over at him. "Are you still leaving on the twenty-sixth?"

"Unfortunately, I have to. I stretched my vacation a bit by coming down on Friday. If I don't go back, the guy who wanted off over New Year's can't leave on time."

"Then I guess you have to go." She'd hold off until then. Somehow.

"We're lucky t'have ye at all," Hamish said. "Canna wait for June."

Zoe turned in her seat. "So the Montana McGavin Invasion is firming up?"

"Aye," Greer said. "Kendra's checkin' into flights. Will ye be able to come, d'ye think?"

"Probably not. I'll be in Milwaukee." Might as well establish that now. Seth had told her Greer liked straight talk. "But I'm sure you'll all have a wonderful time."

"Och, lass, we will for sure, but I was hopin' ye'd consider relocatin' and openin' a studio here."

"I won't be doing that. Milwaukee is my home."

"Well, then that's that, isn't it? I wish ye well."

"Thank you." She peeked at Seth. Was his jaw tight? In any case, he wasn't smiling.

Hamish changed the subject. "Ah, we're nearin' the town. Think our wee village would string garlands across the street, Greer?"

"Could be," Greer said. "I'll ask my friend on the council."

"We're almost there." Seth made a left into a residential area. "Kendra told me to park at the first available space and walk the rest of the way. If you look straight ahead, you'll see the church spire on your right. And people walking in that direction."

"Seth and I went explorin' today," Hamish said. "Drove by this wee kirk. Reminded me of one at home."

Zoe leaned forward. "There's a spot three cars up."

"Thanks." He pulled beyond it and backed neatly into the parallel space.

"One try. Well done, lad." His dad patted him on the shoulder. "Glad it was ye and not myself."

Greer chuckled. "We're all glad of that. We'd be backin' and fillin' for days."

"Och! Not days." He laughed. "Hours, maybe."

Seth met Zoe on her side of the SUV. "Ma and Da, just follow us."

"Aye," Hamish said. "We'll be right behind ye, son."

Zoe looked over her shoulder as they started off. Hamish and Greer were far enough back that they wouldn't hear her if she kept her voice down. "I thought I might as well let your ma know my decision."

He nodded. "It's for the best if you do." His breath fogged the air. "Then she won't get her hopes up about... anything."

"Right." But it was his hopes that made her heart ache. She wrapped her arms around her middle.

"Cold?" He put his arm over her shoulder.

"No, not really. I just..."

His grip tightened. "Yeah, I know." He cleared his throat. "Look at that. They've put luminarias out along the walkway leading to the church. And pine boughs over the doorway."

"Beautiful." Her vision blurred and she blinked back unexpected tears.

"I've never been to a Christmas Eve candlelight ceremony."

"I have."

"How many?"

"Lots. My folks love them." If Aunt Mo had her way, they'd be here at this church next Christmas Eve. So would she. And her baby.

Chances were Seth and his folks would be in a nearby pew. How had something so beautiful become such a nightmare?

27

Seth hadn't been inside a church since he'd been a groomsman for a wedding in Apple Grove a couple of years ago. He wasn't into churches, in general, but this one... he'd be back.

Candles and muted lighting created soft shadows on the stone walls. The arched stained glass windows, lit from the outside, glowed in jewel tones that reflected on the draped altar, the wooden pews, and the people tightly packed into each one.

Ah, some space in a row near the back. He turned toward Ma and Da, pointed toward the vacant section and started toward it. The four of them had to squeeze in to fit. Without prior communication, he and his Da instinctively put the women in the middle.

Zoe leaned toward his ma and said something to her. His ma reached for Zoe's hand and gave it a squeeze.

The soft organ music ended and Pastor Bennett began the service. Godman had transformed into a humble preacher who spoke sincerely about the power of love.

Seth reached for Zoe's hand and slipped his fingers through hers. Pastor Bennett believed love could do anything. But did Zoe love him? Warts and all?

Words from his childhood miraculously came to him as he stood next to Zoe and sang hymns of praise. Beside him, her sweet voice rose with the others. She could sing. He wanted to learn everything about her. Would he get the chance? Pastor Bennett said he would if he loved with all his heart.

As the lights came down even more, the lighting of the candles began. Seth accepted the flame from the woman next to him and touched his candle to Zoe's. "I love you," he murmured.

Her eyes were moist as she met his gaze. Then she turned and touched her candle to his ma's. The service ended with candles flickering and the congregation singing *Silent Night* a cappella.

Zoe didn't sing.

On the way back to the ranch, his folks raved about the beautiful service and the talents of Pastor Bennett, who could have people rolling in the aisles at the GG talent show and filled with love and inspiration as they gathered in his wee church, or kirk, as his ma and da called it.

Zoe put in a word here and there, but she was unnaturally subdued. When he pulled up to the ranch and climbed out to give his folks each a hug, Zoe did the same.

He helped her back in, returned to the driver's seat and closed the door. "Do you want to talk about it?"

"No." Her voice sounded funny, like she was trying not to cry.

"Okay." He gripped the wheel. This wasn't good. They'd always been able to communicate. Now she was clamming up.

He drove in silence through the cold night. Ahead of them, the lights of Main Street twinkled, mocking him with an abundance of good cheer. Christmas Eve. Yay.

"You and your da drove around this afternoon?"

"We did. He wanted to see more of the town. Then we met my brothers, Tansy, Damaris and Damaris's folks for a beer, or a pint, as they say."

"Sounds nice."

"It was. They put pressure on me to move here. Didn't take much. I ended up telling them my plans."

"I'll bet they're eager to help."

"They are. Listen, I appreciate the attempt at polite conversation, but we've never been about that. I can only conclude that I effed up by saying I love you and now we have a bigger problem than we had before."

Silence.

His chest tightened. "Clearly you don't love me back, then."

"I didn't say that."

"No, but your silence speaks volumes."

"Why would I say I love you when all that will do is make things worse?"

"The hell it will!"

"The hell it won't! I'm *leaving Montana*. It's like you're ignoring—"

"Are you kidding? That's all I think about. You going back there in April, living in some lonely apartment, just you and your kid."

"I won't be lonely! I have my parents and my friends and my studio. Even if that weren't the case, are you going to move to Milwaukee and fix that hypothetical situation?"

"No, I'm not."

"Didn't think so. And I'm not staying here, so—"

"Dammit, Zoe, the thought of that baby growing up like I did is—"

"None of your business!"

"It is if I love you! And I love that little munchkin, too! Why won't you even consider—"

"Because my plan existed long before you showed up, buster. I don't need—"

"Obviously! You don't need a stinkin' thing. Especially not me. God, you're stubborn."

"I'm stubborn because I love my child!"

"If you loved your child you'd want them to have a dad. And I'd make a damned good one."

"You think you know everything."

"I know that much." And he was done. With great effort, he kept the needle at the speed limit on the way through town and only punched it a little on the outskirts. He drove Aunt Mo's road carefully, because… ditches.

He pulled into a parking space and she was out of the car before he shut off the engine, racing for the door. He slammed the door and took off after her, managed to catch her when she slipped on the ice and would've gone down.

She shook him off and kept going. She must have dug her key out before she exited the car, because she had the door open in two seconds.

He let her go. Instead of climbing the steps, he stood on the sidewalk and gazed up at the stars. "Okay, Godman. I put my faith in you tonight. So far things aren't looking too good. It's Christmas. Aren't we supposed to have miracles going on?"

Silence.

* * *

Zoe couldn't figure out a way to get out of the McGavin Christmas dinner. If she told Aunt Mo she didn't feel well, her aunt would worry that something was wrong with the baby. She'd probably insist on staying home, too, and maybe even lobby for a trip to the ER for a checkup.

Kendra had invited them to come at two for drinks, munchies, board games and whatever else the McGavins did on Christmas Day before their big holiday meal. At one-forty-five, Zoe gave Seth a quick smile as he helped her into the front passenger seat of the SUV.

He quickly returned the smile and glanced away. He looked like hell. Or maybe nobody else would think so. He'd showered, shaved and put on the Christmas plaid shirt she'd propped against his door early this morning.

He'd fooled Aunt Mo with a wink and a smile when she'd complimented him on the shirt. Her aunt's excitement over spending the afternoon and evening at Wild Creek might have blinded her to the ever-present crease between Seth's brow and the barely masked pain in his eyes. His jaw was tight and his breathing shallow.

She was in no better shape. Her chest ached and her eyes burned. A bag of baby toys had been outside her door this morning and she'd tortured herself by looking through it. She'd worn the gold heart necklace he'd hung on her doorknob because Aunt Mo had likely been a part of that choice and would expect to see her wearing it.

The necklace was lovely—feminine, romantic and a constant reminder of the man who'd given it to her. Not that she needed one. In her brain's network, he was on every channel.

Aunt Mo kept the conversation going for the ride over, which allowed Zoe to coast along speaking only to her aunt, never to Seth. He didn't say anything directly to her, either.

They'd had one stilted exchange at breakfast, under cover of the excited chatter of the guests as they discussed their plans for Christmas Day. He'd thanked her for the shirt and she'd thanked him for the necklace and the baby toys.

Last night's clear skies had given way to clouds and Kendra had chosen to leave the outdoor Christmas lights on. Smoke drifted from the chimney and pickups of every color filled the parking area. A large snowman was under construction in the front yard. Two snowsuit-clad toddlers and several adults were in on it.

Seth pulled up beside the construction area and rolled down his window. "Looking good!"

"Hey, Seth!" Cody waved. "Park that thing and get your butt out here. We need more crew for this operation. You, too, Zoe! I hear you're good with snow!"

"I'll be there in a jiffy!" she called back. Building a snowman would be way better than facing the gathering inside. Except Seth had been asked to help. Oh, well.

He parked and shut off the motor. "Go ahead over if you want, Zoe. I'll help Aunt Mo in with her casserole."

"Okay. Sure." She exited the car while Aunt Mo protested that she could carry in the casserole just fine and Seth should go with Zoe.

But he doesn't want to. Maybe he'd find an excuse to keep from joining in at all. Which wasn't right. It was his family, not hers.

She should have taken the casserole. She glanced back, but he was already climbing the steps to the porch. She hurried over to the front yard.

"Hey, Zoe!" Faith lifted the smallest of the toddlers. "Have you ever met Noel?"

"I don't think so." She smiled at the dark-haired little girl. "Hi, Noel. Merry Christmas."

Noel surveyed her with interest, made a cooing sound and reached toward her neck. The shiny gold had caught her eye.

"No, sweetie." Faith gently intercepted the grab for the necklace. "She loves anything that shines or sparkles."

"I'm sure." Zoe zipped up her parka to remove temptation.

"Pretty necklace. Christmas present?"

"Yes."

"Your aunt, right?"

"Uh, no, Seth."

"Aha! I thought I detected some interest there. Very cool."

"Auntie Faith! Auntie Faith!"

Zoe glanced down and a tow-headed little kid was tugging on Faith's pant leg. "Who's this?"

"Josh. Josh, this is your Auntie Zoe. Can you say hi?"

He looked up. "Hi. I never seed you before."

"I'm new in town."

"Oh." He turned back to Faith. "Auntie Faith, you need to come back *now*. The snowman's getting *big*." He spread his chubby arms. "Noel wants to see!"

Faith grinned. "I'm sure she does. Let's go."

"Let's go!" Josh ran ahead, tripped and plopped in the snow, but scrambled up, undaunted, and kept going. "I get Auntie Faith! I get Noel! And Auntie... Auntie..."

"Zoe!" Zoe called after him. Instant auntie status. Heartwarming.

"Auntie Zoe! She's new."

"Good job, sport." A broad-shouldered cowboy scooped him up. "We're ready to put the eyes on."

"Help me out, Faith," Zoe murmured. "Josh is a Sawyer, right?"

"Yep. That's his dad, Gage, Quinn's middle son. He's married to Emma, the blond lady over there."

"Thanks. You'd think I'd have everyone straight by now."

"Trust me, it takes a while."

"Hey, Faith, I need Noel."

Zoe glanced toward the speaker, who sounded more like Ryker than Cody. It *was* Ryker.

"Noel, wanna go see your Uncle Ryker? I think he has a project for you."

The little girl bounced and cooed before holding out her arms to Ryker.

"Attagirl." Ryker settled her in the crook of his arm. "You get to pick out which carrot we use for the nose." He carried her over to the porch steps.

"Wow," Zoe said. "She went right to him."

"Oh, yeah. She does that with everyone, but she especially loves her uncles. And they love her."

Zoe watched Ryker's tenderness with the little girl as they sorted through the bag together. "That's obvious."

"It's a great feeling, having so many people around who would do anything for your kid. Ryker would go to the mat for Noel. So would any of them."

"That... that must be nice."

"It's fabulous. Did I hear you might be staying?"

"Greer floated a trial balloon, but no, I won't be."

"That's too bad. I've *always* wanted to try yoga. This morning while we were opening presents some of us were talking about it and we have enough for a class just in our family alone."

"You could get a video and get together as a group to practice."

"We might if you won't be opening a studio, but I like having someone with experience on hand. That way you don't learn bad habits."

"We found the right nose!" Ryker came back with Noel, who was vigorously chewing on it. "Better attach it before it gets too mangled."

Josh dissolved into a fit of giggles. "Noel's eating the nose! Noel's eating the nose!"

Zoe smiled. "How old is he?"

"He turned two this fall. Precocious little guy. Noel just turned one."

Zoe hesitated. "I guess the word's out that I'm preggers."

"I heard that. How far?"

"A little more than five months. I'm barely showing now, but soon it'll be obvious."

"It's none of my business, but is the father—"

"He's in Wisconsin. I'm looking forward to raising the baby on my own."

"Wow. I have no idea what that would be like." She grinned. "With this bunch, that's darned near impossible."

28

With the snowman finished, the group started on a snow woman. Zoe got in on the ground floor of the construction. Partway through Seth showed up and was razzed for being a slacker.

He dived into the action and the awkwardness between them slowly melted. She could hardly maintain her distance when they were sharing the task of adding snow to the chest of an already well-endowed snow woman.

She smoothed her side. "I think that's enough."

"Mine's bigger."

"So shave some off."

He flashed her a grin. "Or you could add some on."

She laughed and rolled her eyes. "Men and their fixations."

"I know. We're terrible." He glanced at her. "Having fun?"

"Yeah. You?"

"Yep. I—oh, look, here comes Quinn. Hey, Quinn, we need your artistic eye over here!"

"I'm on it."

Kendra followed him out and headed straight for the toddlers. "Wanna come in for a snack, kids?"

"Snack, snack!" Josh hopped up and down while Noel stared up at her looking uncertain.

Kendra crouched down. "Do you want a snack, Noel? Gramma Greer, Grandpa Hamish and Gramma Mo are fixing something yummy for you."

"She wants a snack," Josh announced. "Let's go."

Seth moved closer to Zoe. "Cute, huh?"

"Adorable." She met his gaze. Laughter, warmth and love shone in his eyes.

And something deep inside shifted. Her breath stuttered. She coughed into her hand to cover her reaction. "You know what? I need to warm up a bit, myself."

A spark of hope flickered in his eyes. "Want me to come in with—"

"No, that's okay. There's just something... I'll see you in a bit."

"All right." Confusion doused the sparkle in his eyes. "See you soon."

"Uh-huh." She couldn't explain. Not yet. She followed Kendra, who had a child on each hip as she mounted the porch steps. "I'll get the door for you."

"Thanks, Zoe." She toed off her boots and kicked them toward the pile collecting on the porch.

"Is there somewhere I could make a phone call in private?"

"Sure thing. My office is the first room on the left."

Zoe took off her boots and added them to the pile before stepping inside and closing the door. Shoving her gloves in her pocket, she unzipped her parka and threw back the hood as she walked quickly through the living room and down the hall.

Kendra's office door was closed, probably to keep Josh from going in and playing with delicate electronics. Heart racing, Zoe stepped inside and shut the door.

Hanging her parka on the back of Kendra's office chair, she pulled her phone out of the pocket of her jeans. Danica's number was on her speed dial.

She answered immediately. "Hey, Merry Christmas! Didn't expect to hear from you today." Voices in the background sounded like a gathering was in progress. "What's up?"

Shoot. This was a lousy time to call. "I wanted to talk to you about something important, but you're clearly in the middle of your celebration. I don't want to—"

"No, no, it's fine. Nothing critical going on. What do you need?"

"What if I offered you the option of buying the studio on a payment plan you could handle?"

Danica gasped. "Buy it from you? Why?"

Adrenalin rushed through her system and she began to shake. "I've decided to stay in Eagles Nest and open a studio here."

"Wow! That's *huge.* What brought that on?"

"A whole bunch of things." And one beautiful man. "There's no way I can swing it unless I sell the studio there, and I'd hate to see someone take over who doesn't know what they're doing. Our students are awesome and they deserve to have—"

"I'll do it."

"You will? Seriously?"

"Seriously. I'm sad as hell that you're not coming back, but man, this is such an opportunity. The studio is doing so great. I'd be a fool to say no. I'll talk to my bank in the morning about a loan so we can settle on a payment plan."

"That's great." Her voice quivered and she took a quick breath. "We can work out the details after the first of the year, but—"

"Or sooner!" Danica laughed. "I don't know what your schedule looks like between Christmas and New Year's, but I'd love to start the paperwork ASAP. This is life-changing, Zoe. I feel like I just won an award or something. Thank you, thank you, thank you. What an awesome Christmas!"

She took a shaky breath. "You can say that again."

"What an awesome Christmas!"

Zoe grinned. "Yeah, sure is. Listen, I'll let you get back to your celebration and we'll talk tomorrow, okay?"

"Okay! Merry Christmas! Bye!"

"Bye." Heart racing, she disconnected the call and tucked the phone in her jacket pocket with shaking hands. Step One, completed. Now for Step Two.

The noise level outside the door had increased. Sounded like everyone had come inside. Well, that was perfect, wasn't it?

After taking several deep breaths, she opened the door, stepped into the hall and headed toward the packed living room. Seth stood over by the Christmas tree holding Rhys, who was playing peek-a-boo while Zane watched with a proud dad smile.

She couldn't say who was having more fun. Rhys clapped his pudgy hands over his eyes, then flung his hands aside, whacking Seth in the face. Seth's laughter mingled with baby giggles. Then the routine began again.

Her breath caught. She'd almost let this wonderful man go. She'd almost allowed the ties to her past to sabotage what promised to be an amazing future for her child, for Seth, for her.

"Hey, Zoe!" Bryce came toward her with a bottle. "When I found out you'd be here, I brought you some of our GG sarsaparilla."

"Thank you so much! That's very thoughtful." She took the bottle. "I'll just set it here for a minute. I have something I need to do." She found a coaster and set the bottle on the nearest end table. Then she started across the room, her attention on Seth.

Eventually he noticed her approach and turned in her direction, a question in his gaze. Rhys patted his new friend's cheeks as if to coax him back to the game.

Conversation and laughter swirled around her... until she halted in front of Seth and dropped to one knee. Then even the kids grew quiet.

Seth's eyes widened.

"I'll take Rhys." Zane scooped his son out of Seth's arms.

Zoe's heart beat so loud her ears buzzed. She grasped Seth's calloused hand in both of hers. "I love you with all my heart."

He gasped. "Zoe…"

"I love you with all my heart and I want to live with you and our baby in a log house in Eagles Nest. Will you marry me?"

His stunned expression transformed into radiant joy. "Hallelujah!" He tugged her to her feet and into his arms as the room erupted with shouts and whistles and applause.

"Saints be praised!" Hamish shouted.

"Champagne!" Kendra cried out. "We need champagne!"

"And McGavin's Pale Ale!" Rory said.

"And sarsaparilla!" Bryce added with a laugh.

As family members scurried around gathering the appropriate toasting drinks and glasses for the champagne drinkers, Seth drew her close and gazed into her eyes. "What's happened?"

"I'm selling the studio to Danica. We'll start the paperwork tomorrow."

"I can't believe it."

"Believe it." She smiled. "Because it's Christmas."

"You changed your mind because it's Christmas?"

"No. I changed my mind because only an idiot walks away from true love. Especially on Christmas."

"Thank God." He cupped her cheek. "I love you so much."

"And I love you back."

"Warts and all?"

"What?"

"It's just something Da said. If I ever found a lass who loved me warts and all, I needed to hang onto her."

"Then you'd better hang onto me."

"I intend to." He lowered his head. "Best Christmas ever."

"Yep." As his lips settled on hers, she was sure of it.

A Note from Vicki

I've adored writing the McGavin Brothers series, so much so that I couldn't let it go until now. I've also adored the lovely and heartwarming comments you've sent me about these books. Clearly you've fallen in love with Eagles Nest, too, and the amazing folks who live there.

Many of you have said you want to move to Eagles Nest. Me, too! With every book, I've relished returning to that friendly little town, visiting with Kendra at Wild Creek Ranch, sipping tea with Aunt Mo at The Nesting Place, ordering a slice of pie at Pie in the Sky, and savoring a mug of McGavin's Pale Ale at the Guzzling Grizzly.

Consequently, although I'll be moving on to the next series, I won't be going that far away! Apple Grove, Seth's former home town, is a mere four-hour drive from Eagles Nest. As I begin a new adventure with The Buckskin Brotherhood, I promise we'll stay connected to our favorite Eagles Nesters!

Many thanks for reading and loving The McGavin Brothers. It's been an honor and a pleasure to share these stories with you. I look forward to continuing our special connection with The Buckskin Brotherhood!

Matt Ramsey gets roped in by a runaway bride in SWEET-TALKING COWBOY, the first book in the Buckskin Brotherhood series!

* * * * *

Passengers filed off the plane and Matt watched for Lucy. How much had she changed? At nineteen, she'd been lithe and toned from yoga and volleyball. Hard to resist. But he'd done it.

A brunette being carried along by the stream of passengers like a leaf in the current captured his attention. She wore a Seattle Mariners zip-up sweatshirt over a long white dress that brushed the ground as she walked. A wedding dress? Surely not.

Then the woman looked at him and her blue eyes flashed with recognition. Picking up her voluminous skirts, she hurried in his direction. "Hi, Matt."

"Lucy?"

"I know, I know. I'm a disaster. Let's just get out of here."

'Where's your husband?"

"Fortunately, I don't have one. I learned the truth about that lying piece of cow poop before it was too late. I just need the peaceful surroundings of the Buckskin." Her voice trembled. "Once I have that, everything will be okay."

He resisted the urge to gather her into his arms. "Let's go fetch your luggage."

"I left it at the church."

"What?"

"Didn't want it. I bought that stuff to wear on my honeymoon with Swamp Thing. Mom can donate it to charity."

"Lucy! You ran out on your wedding?"

Her chin lifted and her eyes glittered. "Damn straight I did. Jumped in the limo, took off for Sea-Tac, got the last stand-by seat." She'd given him that same look six years ago when she'd told him to go to hell.

"Nobody came after you?"

Her gaze dropped to the floor. "I sort of had a meltdown and screamed at them not to follow me."

"What about your folks? Won't they be worried?"

"I texted them from the limo and told them I was coming here and I'd explain later."

"Then your... fiancé... won't be..."

"If I never see that lying louse again I'll be eternally grateful. Augghhh!!" She shook her hands in distress. When she glanced up, pain had replaced the defiance in her eyes. "Let's just go."

"My truck's in the garage." Putting a hand at her waist, he guided her to the outside door. Then he caught her arm. "Wait. That sweatshirt isn't enough." He took off his jacket. "Put this on."

"No, you need it."

"The vest will do fine."

"It won't. I—"

"The sooner you put on my coat the sooner we'll get out of here."

"All right."

He helped her into it and waited until she'd fastened the buttons. "Let's go." He rested a hand on her shoulder as they walked out of the terminal and across to the parking garage under an icy blue winter sky. She wasn't married. She hadn't found happiness, after all. What had those six years done to his Lucy?

Not that she was his. Not by a long shot. But how had she guessed so wrong when choosing a husband? Then again, six years ago she'd wanted him.

New York Times bestselling author Vicki Lewis Thompson's love affair with cowboys started with the Lone Ranger, continued through Maverick, and took a turn south of the border with Zorro. She views cowboys as the Western version of knights in shining armor, rugged men who value honor, honesty and hard work. Fortunately for her, she lives in the Arizona desert, where broad-shouldered, lean-hipped cowboys abound. Blessed with such an abundance of inspiration, she only hopes that she can do them justice.

For more information about this prolific author, visit her website and sign up for her newsletter. She loves connecting with readers.

VickiLewisThompson.com